Letters to God

Letters to God

A NOVEL

PATRICK DOUGHTIE
AND JOHN PERRY

ZONDERVAN.com/
AUTHORTRACKER
follow your favorite authors

ZONDERVAN

Letters to God

This title is also available as a Zondervan ebook.
Visit www.zondervan.com/ebooks.

This title is also available in a Zondervan audio edition.
Visit www.zondervan.fm.

Requests for information should be addressed to:

Zondervan, *Grand Rapids, Michigan 49530*

Library of Congress Cataloging-in-Publication Data

Doughtie, Patrick-
Letters to God : from the major motion picture / Patrick Doughtie and John Perry.
p. cm.
Summary: Inspired by the major motion picture Letters to God, this novel is for readers eager to read more of this inspiring story. Tyler, a nine-year-old boy, is stricken with incurable brain cancer and begins to write letters to God. He turns his suffering into spiritual lessons for his widowed mother, his embittered adolescent brother, and a troubled postman. This story of hope will help readers from all walks work toward greater understanding of God's presence and care.
ISBN 978-0-310-32765-3 (softcover)
1. Brain—Cancer—Patients—Fiction. 2. Epistolary fiction. I. Perry, John, 1952- II. Title.
PS3604.O923L48 2010
813'.6—dc22 2009051237

Published in association with the literary agency of Wolgemuth & Associates, Inc.

Interior design: Michelle Espinoza

Printed in the United States of America

10 11 12 13 14 15 16 /DCI/ 22 21 20 19 18 17 16 15 14 13 12 11 10 9 8

To
Savanah and Brendan Doughtie,
Olivia Perry, and Charles Perry here,
and Tyler there

Letters to God

Patrick

Patrick Doherty fished around in the desk drawer for a pencil without taking his eyes off the page. Not that he was in a hurry; he just never wanted to waste any of his precious quiet time. A small circle of light fell from a lamp in the corner where he sat. The street outside was still dark, and his wife, Maddy, still slept, burrowed deep under the covers, her breathing slow and regular. Very soon a high-energy three-year-old would come bounding into the bedroom and quiet time would be over. As much as he loved his son's morning hello, he wanted to finish a couple of things first.

Rereading a sentence, Patrick underlined three lines in his Bible and jotted a thought out to the side, where the margins were already peppered with years' worth of questions, comments, and references. To him it made sense to have his notes handy like that.

Patrick finished reading, then cracked open the window blinds enough to send a few thin parallel strips of dawn light across the desktop. Sliding open the lap drawer, he took out a notebook with a handwritten title on the front: *Letters to God.* He flipped through to the first blank page and sat thinking for a minute before starting to write rapidly, the words tumbling out almost faster than he could get them down. He paused, read over what he'd written, and smiled, looking at his wife and wishing she'd open her eyes and look back. He loved her eyes.

As he started writing again, he heard little feet scurrying down the hall and a voice chirping, "Rise and shine! Rise and shine!"

"Hey, Tiger," Patrick said.

"Hey, Dad," Tyler Doherty answered from the bedroom doorway, then looked at the lump in the bed. "Hey, Mom! Time to get up!"

The lump rustled only a little. "Not yet, sweetie. Mommy needs more sleep."

"But I'm hungry."

"Don't worry, Ty," the lump answered groggily. "You won't starve to death. Mommy'll be up in a minute."

Ty pattered over to the desk in the corner where his father sat and looked out through the blinds. The sun rising behind the big moss-covered live oaks that lined the street gave them long, crisp shadows on the pavement. Ty liked watching the sun come up. He saw people walking their dogs on the sidewalk and a car backing out of the driveway in front of a blue house across the way. A few doors down, his friend Samantha's dad came out to get the paper. Turning to look at his dad, Ty was at eye level with the open notebook.

"Whatcha doing, Daddy?"

"Writing."

"Writing what?"

"I'm writing a letter to God."

"Wow!" Ty was impressed. "Will he write you back?"

How, at six thirty in the morning, could he explain this to a three-year-old, even a very sharp three-year-old?

"Well, no … I mean, yes, in a way, Son."

Ty furrowed his little brow. Maddy was up now, and Patrick looked at her with a silent plea for help.

"You're on your own, messenger boy," she said to Patrick with a chuckle as she headed down the hall to root Ben out of bed. Ty's eleven-year-old brother was the certified baghound in the family.

"When I write a letter to God, it's my way of talking to him. I'm praying, really."

Ty thought it over. "Why don't you just talk to him then?"

"Well, I've always had a hard time praying, and it's easier for me to write him a letter. Sometimes he answers them, but not with another letter exactly. You see?"

Tyler shook his head.

"You will, you will." Patrick laughed, ran his hand over Ty's light blond hair, then held out his arms for Ty to jump into them. "I love you, Ty."

"I love you, Daddy."

Glancing at the bedside alarm, Patrick set Ty on the bed and stood. "I've got to get ready for work, Son. We'll talk more about it later. Go help your mom wake Ben up for school."

"Okay!" With a yelp of excitement, Ty raced through the hall, screaming, "Ben! Get up!" Sliding to a halt in his older brother's bedroom doorway, he waved the door back and forth, then banged it open against the wall. "Rise and shine!"

Two blue eyes topped by a nest of dark hair peered out from under the sheet. "Get lost, dork," came a voice from somewhere in the pile.

Ty pivoted on one foot and bolted back to his parents' room. It was empty; Mom was downstairs starting breakfast and Dad was in the bathroom with the door closed. Ty could hear the shower running. He walked over to the desk where his dad's notebook still lay open. This was the perfect time to draw Daddy a picture! Ty grabbed the pencil and made a circle beside two stick figures, one larger than the other; it was him and his dad and the sunrise. Hearing the shower shut off, he dropped the pencil in the middle of the notebook and ran giggling from the room.

Patrick appeared wrapped in a bathrobe, briskly rubbing his wet hair with a towel. He was an inch or so over six feet, though his muscular shoulders and athletic posture made him seem even taller. Physical labor had kept his body lean, only a few pounds heavier than his playing weight a dozen years ago on the way to a baseball scholarship. His freshly shaven face was lightly lined, tanned and ruddy from years of working outdoors, the deep blue eyes framed by thick dark hair. Ben had his hair and eyes. Ty was brown-eyed and blond like his mother.

Patrick looked toward the sound of giggles and footsteps in the hall, then at the desk. Picking up his notebook, he saw the scribbles on top of that morning's letter. His frown of irritation changed to a wide grin as he read the last sentence he'd written: "And Lord, all I ask is for a little sunshine today, something to make it a little better than yesterday." There his sunshine was, taking up nearly the whole page.

"Thank you, Lord," he said, looking upward. "I haven't even left the house yet this morning, and you've already answered my prayer."

As he headed for the kitchen a few minutes later, the smell of cinnamon toast—the boys' favorite—met him on the stairs. The Doherty home was the airy, rambling kind of old house that some people called "four square," with a bedroom upstairs in each corner and a big stair hall in the middle. The high ceilings helped keep it cool during the Orlando summers, and big windows let in lots of light in the wintertime. Patrick was dressed for "the office"—jeans, a work shirt, heavy boots, and a baseball cap, to which he would shortly add a tool belt and nail apron. His strong, calloused hands came not from pushing papers behind a desk but from long days as a carpenter, carrying, cutting, measuring, and fitting lumber, swinging a sixteen-ounce hammer, and climbing around construction sites.

Passing by Ben and Ty at the breakfast table, he reached for a mug of steaming coffee waiting on the counter. Expertly juggling the mug, he took a Thermos and lunchbox from Maddy's outstretched hands, gave her a kiss on the lips, and headed for the door.

"Hey, Dad," Ben hollered after him, "you're gonna make it to my football game today, right?"

Patrick stopped in his tracks and cut his eyes over to Maddy. Behind the children and out of their sight, she held up an outstretched palm, wiggling all five fingers.

"Uh, yeah. It starts at five, right?"

"Right!" Ben said, grinning.

"Wouldn't miss it!"

Maddy flagged for his attention. "You don't have to work tonight?"

"I'll be there." He shot her a look that said, "Don't you worry about it; I'll take care of things," then a quick smile in Ben's direction as he continued out the door. "I love you guys."

"I love you too," the chorus answered, and he was gone. They heard his truck start then watched him drive across in front of the house and out of sight.

He hadn't wanted that second job working nights for a janitorial service. It took him away from supper time and evenings with his family, and what little time he was home he felt bushed. But he didn't see any choice. Even though new homes were going up all over south Florida and the carpentry business was booming, he couldn't seem to get ahead on his construction salary. "Make my own mess by day, clean up somebody else's mess by night" was the way he put it. At least the night work was physically easy even if it was boring: sweeping, mopping, and emptying trash at a bank downtown.

At 7:30 a.m. sharp, Patrick pulled into the job site, a new house on a big lot at the edge of town, and parked in a row of trucks shaded by a cluster of date palms. Before grabbing his tool belt, he flipped down the sun visor where a favorite picture, the four of them at the beach, was slipped under a rubber band. He nodded at it as he opened the door. "It's all for you guys," he said and headed across the lot and around pallets of construction materials to his table saw.

Patrick liked carpentry work and knew he had a knack for it. He liked the physical part of the job, spending the day outside, moving around, breathing fresh air. He never knew how so many people in the world could spend the day sitting behind a desk with a tie on.

He'd hoped to slip away a few minutes early for Ben's game, but with all the rain the last couple of weeks he was behind schedule and just couldn't manage it. By the time he finally headed for the field, the first drive of the second quarter was under way and Hill Middle School had the ball on their own forty-four.

Ben popped his head up out of the huddle of eleven- and twelve-year-olds and scanned the bleachers. *He said he'd be here.* He looked at his mother. As Ty jumped up and down beside her, she met his gaze with a big thumbs-up. She hoped Patrick would make the game, but it was getting late.

"Doherty, listen up!" The quarterback gave Ben a smack on the shoulder pad and he stuck his head back into the circle. "Pro right, student body left. Ready? Break!" With a grunt and a hand clap, the team jogged toward the line of scrimmage. Taking his place in the backfield, Ben suddenly couldn't remember whether it was student body right or student body left.

"Hey!" he said in a hoarse whisper to the fullback taking his stance beside him. "Right or left?" The quarterback barked off the cadence. Out of the corner of his eye, a movement caught Ben's attention. He knew that shape, that walk, instantly. *He's here. He made it.*

"It's left." Ben turned his head and stared blankly at the fullback. "Left!" the stocky youngster said again.

"Hike!"

Ben swept left, looked over his right shoulder, and saw the football sailing at him. Making the catch, he darted around the defense, picked up a blocker, and pounded a good dozen yards into enemy territory before two tacklers finally brought him down. Scrambling to his feet, he tossed the ball to the referee. He looked toward the stands and saw his dad watching from the sideline, applauding vigorously with his hands high over his head. He gave Ben a thumbs-up, then pointed toward the sky. Ben sent the same signals back.

From her seat in the front row of bleachers, Maddy spotted her husband and caught his exchange with Ben. Ty saw him too, and before Maddy could grab him he darted off to greet him. Maddy followed Ty with her eyes as he scurried to his father, clutching him around the knees. Patrick hoisted his son into the air and hugged him close. Maddy could hear them both laughing even from where she sat. Patrick waved at her, then, with Ty in his arms, picked his way back to where she was sitting.

As the three of them took their places, Maddy squeezed Patrick's arm. "I'm so glad you got here." Her wavy dark blonde hair blew in the breeze and the sun brought out the freckles on her nose. Every time Patrick saw her, he thought she was more beautiful than the time before. He especially liked that mischievous upturn at the corners of her mouth.

"Me too," Patrick answered. "I wouldn't have missed it, but I can't stay long."

She saw the weariness in his eyes. Working two jobs was such a drain on him. "Why don't you call in and say you'll be a little late tonight?"

"I'd love to," he sighed. "But I can't. You know that."

"I know."

The three of them watched the rest of the second quarter together, Patrick and Maddy holding hands and Ty on his dad's lap. As the clock ran out and the whistle sounded, Patrick looked at his watch. He sat Ty on the seat beside him and stood up.

"Tell Ben I love him and that he played an awesome game. Tell him that run was fantastic." As Ben jogged toward the sideline, he saw his father leaving. Catching his eye, he gave him a thumbs-up and pointed to the sky. Patrick signaled back.

"Daddy, I want to go with you," Tyler said, grabbing him around the legs. "Pleeeease?"

"Not this time, Tiger, but some day soon. I promise you I could use the help." He mussed Tyler's hair, then put his arm around Maddy's shoulder and pulled her to him. "Good-bye, love," he said. "See you tonight." He gave her a peck on the lips, disappeared into the halftime crowd, and was gone.

It took him longer than he expected to get to his night job, and he hoped he could slide in without the shift manager noticing. Gary was a sourpuss to start with, and a stickler for punctuality on top of that. He did not like his people being tardy. They met in the hallway.

"You're late," Gary grumped, tapping his wristwatch.

"I know. I'm sorry. I'll make it up at the end of the night."

"You certainly will." Gary walked stiffly away as Patrick headed toward the equipment closet.

It was going to be a long night. Still, at least he had gotten to see part of Ben's game. Yes, he was ten minutes late for work, but it was worth the snide remark to have been there for that fabulous run. He hadn't been able to eat dinner at home, though, and he missed that. Time with his family was so precious; he chafed at every minute he was away from them.

One good thing about his night job was that it gave him time to think. Days on the construction site were all action and noise, but at the bank after hours he could reflect on his life and how, in spite of the challenges and mistakes of the past, the future looked really promising. He knew he had God to thank for all the joy his wife and children brought him. He knew too that when God had a message for him, he often sent it through Maddy's mother. Olivia—the kids called her Granna—was the one who had taught him about Jesus Christ and who convinced him of the value of passing that faith along to his sons. She was relentless but she was right. Patrick had long since lost count of how many times his faith had gotten him through struggles and hardships that would have swamped him otherwise.

It was twelve thirty when he turned off the buffer and critically surveyed the lobby floor, stripped, waxed, polished, and shining like glass. It was too late to call home; Maddy would be sound asleep by now. In six hours he'd have a three-year-old bouncing on his chest and would be starting the whole routine over again.

Weary to the bone, he climbed into his truck, already thinking of his quiet house, warm sheets, and his wife asleep in the bed beside him. He headed onto the familiar two-lane road that led to his neighborhood, listening to the radio to stay alert. He ran his hand down his face, relieved that the long day was over at last.

Stretching out one arm, he bumped the sun visor above his head, knocking loose something that fluttered down in front of his face. The beach photo. He'd be careful not to step on it. He'd have to remember to pick it up after he got to the house. Couldn't go feeling around for it in the dark.

He'd only taken his eyes off the road for an instant, but looking ahead now he saw a car straight ahead in his lane, headlights framing his windshield and closing fast. *Where'd this guy come from?* Reflexively he jerked the wheel to the right with both hands. Too late. The vehicles hit head-on with a dull, metallic crunch. Patrick's pickup flipped, spun, hit a tree, and came to rest upside-down in a ditch. The other vehicle, an SUV, stayed upright on the road, its front end demolished to the firewall, windows broken, front tires in shreds.

Patrick came to consciousness awash in pain, his legs throbbing, the nerves in his back pulsing like electric shocks. He opened his eyes and saw that he was upside-down, suspended by his seat belt, looking out through the broken and bloody windshield. The cab was crushed in every direction, smashed around his head and torso, leaving only inches between his body and outcroppings of twisted, broken metal. Weakly he grabbed the steering wheel and tried to pull himself around, but the motion sent searing jolts of pain through his body and he let go of the wheel with a scream. His legs were caught under the dashboard, which was jammed up against his chest. Other than the pain, he had no feeling anywhere. There was blood but he couldn't tell where it came from.

Drifting in and out, Patrick didn't know how long he dangled there before he heard voices and saw lights. A face appeared through a gap in the wreckage. "Don't worry," it said, "we'll get you out. You're going to be all right." He saw a DayGlo green coat and a fireman's hat.

"Call Maddy, please, call my wife," Patrick managed to say. He felt something sticky on his arms. Lifting them to his face, he could see by the rescue lights that they were covered in blood. He closed his eyes and the light went away. Soon the sound went away too.

Manslaughter

At first Maddy thought it was the alarm clock. How could it be six thirty already? She slapped at it several times but the racket continued. Roused from a deep sleep, she stared bleary-eyed at the numbers. One thirty. "Honey?" she said, feeling for the pillow beside her. "Patrick?" His side of the bed was empty.

It was the phone. She picked it up warily. "Hello?"

"Mrs. Madalynn Doherty?"

"Speaking."

"This is the emergency room duty nurse at Memorial Medical Center."

Maddy was suddenly wide awake, every nerve engaged.

"Your husband has been in a traffic accident. He was brought here by LifeFlight."

"Is it serious?"

"You can talk to the doctor when you get here. But you need to come right away."

"Okay. I'm coming." Moving on autopilot, Maddy slipped into a jogging suit and ran a comb through her hair. She'd call her mother to stay with the boys. No, she couldn't wait that long. The boys could go with her.

"Mom?" Ben was standing in the bedroom doorway in a T-shirt and boxers. "What's going on?" His voice was groggy with sleep, his hair spiking in every direction. She looked at him, tying her shoes. "Where are you going?" He glanced around. "Where's Dad?"

"Your dad's been in an accident." She fought to keep in control. She didn't want to scare the boys unnecessarily. Maybe it wasn't all that bad. "Wake up your brother and get some shoes on. We have to go."

Ben rushed to Ty's room and shook him awake. "Tyler, come on, wake up! We have to go!"

"Leave me alone," Ty warned. Ben stooped down over his brother, gathered him up, and started down the hall holding him in his arms. "I'm telling Mom!" Ty yelled. The two of them met their mother at the top of the stairs. "Mom—!"

"It's okay, Ty. We're all going for a ride."

Putting his brother down, Ben ducked into his room and pulled on jeans and a shirt while Maddy helped Ty get dressed, then carried him down the stairs with Ben following. They piled into the van, pulling out onto the empty street as Maddy reached for her cell phone. She'd have her mother meet them at the hospital.

By the time the gurney carrying Patrick Doherty came banging through the double doors of the ER, nobody who'd treated him on the medical chopper thought he would make it. His legs were crushed from the waist down. He had serious internal injuries. Most critical was the swelling of his brain that, if it hadn't already killed him, would likely make him an invalid for life. Yet somehow, miraculously, he was still hanging on.

The gurney wheeled past a second patient, the driver of the

other car, who'd arrived by ambulance while the rescue workers were still trying to cut Patrick out of the remains of his truck. The man had a butterfly bandage on his forehead and eleven stitches in his left hand. He sat on the edge of an examining table surrounded by a doctor, a nurse, and two policemen.

"So you haven't had anything to drink tonight," one of the policemen was saying.

"I swear, officer, I haven't had a drop," the man answered. He was in his early sixties with a head of luxuriant iron-gray hair. He wore a yellow silk sport shirt. "Not a drop all day."

The policemen knew better. The dull expression and unsteady walk could have been caused by the wreck, but they didn't think so.

"We found eight empty beer cans in the back floor of your car," said the other officer, matter-of-factly.

"It must have been the kids," the man explained.

"Then you won't mind taking a breathalyzer test, will you?"

"Hey, wait a minute. I told you I haven't been drinking. Why waste the taxpayers' money ... ?" Their conversation continued as a medical team clustered around Patrick, motionless on an examining table, bristling with tubes and sensors.

Outside, following the blue neon "Emergency" arrows, Maddy drove up near the entrance and parked as close as she could. She and the boys raced through the automatic doors and up to the desk, anxious and out of breath.

"My husband's Patrick Doherty. I got a call saying there'd been an accident."

"I'll find out where he is," a nurse behind the desk answered.

"Just a minute." She scanned a computer screen, tapped a few strokes, read something, then tapped again.

"Hurry, please," Maddy said. Eyes still on the screen, the nurse waved her hand in a *yeah, don't worry about it* way. Maddy fidgeted nervously, shifting her weight, tapping her fingers on the counter. The boys watched in silence.

"He's in surgery, ma'am," the nurse reported, her voice emotionless.

"What's wrong with him? How bad is he hurt?" Her voice was getting louder as she felt the panic rising.

"This is all the information I have, ma'am. I'll notify the doctor that you're here, and he'll be with you as soon as he can."

She was about to say, "I want to know something *now*!" when the entrance doors slid open and her mother marched briskly in, moving fast despite her ample figure, dressed in pajamas, sequined slippers, and a bathrobe printed with pink cabbage roses. Her hair—strawberry blonde mixed with gray—was in rollers, each one wrapped in toilet paper, which made them easier to sleep on.

The spectacle startled Maddy so much that she forgot for a moment how mad and afraid she was. "Mother!" she squeaked. "The least you could have done was take the toilet paper off your head!"

"Who cares about toilet paper!" her mother declared. "How's Patrick?"

"I don't know. They won't tell me anything."

"Come over here and sit down." She herded her daughter and grandsons to an empty row of chairs in the waiting area. The two women sat down while the boys stood in front of them, guided into place by their grandmother's steady hands. "Let's pray," she said. They all nodded. Of course that would be the first thing she'd think to do.

As they bowed their heads, a policeman walked into the room carrying a small box. "Is there a Mrs. Doherty here?" he asked.

"Here!" Maddy jumped to her feet. "I'm Maddy Doherty."

He motioned her over to where he was standing so the two of them could talk in relative privacy. "I'm sorry about your husband. These are his personal belongings we recovered at the scene before they towed his truck." He held up the box.

Maddy held her hands out reflexively and took the box. "What happened?"

"Your husband was in a head-on collision with another vehicle. Because of the damage to the cab, we had to cut him out of his truck. The other driver is being treated for minor injuries. He is going to be arrested for driving under the influence and vehicular manslaughter. We found a pile of empty beer cans in his car, and he flunked his sobriety test—point-one-one and the legal limit is point-oh-eight. He had five or six drinks for sure, maybe more."

The color drained from Maddy's face. Her mother saw her stumble, then regain her balance. Olivia motioned for the boys to stay put and walked over to where Maddy and the officer stood.

"Manslaughter?" Maddy repeated. Her mouth would hardly form the word. "I don't understand. Was there someone who died? The nurse just told me my husband was in surgery—"

Now it was the officer's turn to blanch. He looked at Granna, then at Maddy, then back at Granna. "Oh, uh, ma'am, I'm so sorry. I shouldn't have said that. I don't really know how your husband is. It's just that he looked so bad when we got him out, I didn't think he'd make it. I'm—I—"

"Not make it?!" Maddy felt the panic coming again. The tears welled up.

"Maddy!" her mother called out. "Honey, he doesn't know anything. He's just trying to help." She gestured with her head. "The kids!" she added quietly.

Maddy looked across at her sons, frightened and frozen in their seats. They could see but not hear what was happening; they didn't know what to think, what to do.

"Thank you, officer," Granna said. "We appreciate your help." The policeman left quickly, a look of genuine relief on his face at the chance to get out of there.

"Let's all go get something to eat," Granna said, loudly enough for the boys to hear, as she started for the snack bar. "Tell them we're in there," she said to the nurse behind the desk, pointing through the doorway.

Mother and daughter sat side by side at a table, untouched cups of vending-machine coffee in front of them. The boys had been gobbling candy bars and other junk that was usually off-limits, courtesy of their grandmother. It was 3:30 in the morning and the four of them waited alone. Finally the door opened and a doctor walked slowly in. He was middle-aged, slightly overweight, and absolutely exhausted. He wore surgical scrubs with a green cap tied around his head and a mask pulled down around his neck. Maddy walked toward him.

"Are you Mrs. Doherty?" the doctor asked wearily.

"Yes. How is he?"

"Would you come with me, please?" He turned and opened the door for her. They walked back into the empty waiting room and sat down in the first row of chairs. The doctor folded his arms in silence, gathering his thoughts.

"Your husband suffered a traumatic brain injury," he began. "The swelling could not be hemostatically arrested. He suffered concurrently from deep pulmonary lacerations caused by a dozen fractured ribs consistent with a deceleration event of this magnitude."

Maddy stared at the doctor, motionless, tears streaming down her face. "Can you say that in English, please?"

The doctor pressed his lips together and raised his fingertips to them, then cradled his chin in his thumb and forefinger. He looked at the ground; he looked up into her eyes.

"Mrs. Doherty, I'm sorry. Your husband didn't make it."

The Unfillable Void

The steel gray autumn sky cast its diffused light on a casket covered with roses, a tiny island of brilliant red in a sea of mourners' black. Off a little to one side, Maddy sat with her mother and children under a blue awning, the tears and mascara streaming down from behind oversized sunglasses. It seemed like she hadn't closed her eyes once since Patrick died, only wiped them and wiped some more until there couldn't possibly be any tears left. What little sleep she got was broken by an endless string of phone calls from well-meaning friends, church members, and Patrick's coworkers.

Ty sat beside his mother, restless and excited, not really understanding what was going on except that his mother was very sad and his father was gone somewhere. On Maddy's other side, Ben leaned forward in his seat, still consumed by raw shock, a numb expression on his face. He stared at the roses and the glossy finish of the casket beneath as Pastor Andy finished his brief remarks with a Bible verse: "The Lord is nigh unto all them that call upon him, to all that call upon him in truth. He will fulfill the desire of them that fear him: he also will hear their cry, and will save them." He looked at Maddy to underscore the words.

She was so grateful for his kindness during these past few days. Maddy knew Psalm 145. Though she'd read it before, it had never hit her like it did now.

And yet, lips pressed hard together in a straight line, she wondered, *Will he hear my cry? What about the cries of my children? Has he heard Ty asking constantly when his daddy is coming home? Heard Ben sobbing his heart out late at night when he assumes everybody's asleep? I don't think so.*

Pastor Andy closed his Bible and bowed his head. In silence, cemetery workers in dark green uniforms picked up a pair of sturdy woven straps and began lowering the casket into the ground.

Ben jumped to his feet. "Dad!" he shouted, his reedy preteen voice cracking. The smooth polished rectangle disappearing into the ground was his last physical connection with his father.

"Dad!" The crowd turned to look at him. His mother and Granna reached up from opposite sides to sit him back down. Slumping into the rickety folding chair with a clatter, he started to cry. Maddy leaned over and put her arm over his shoulders.

Hearing his brother, Ty sat bolt upright, looking around excitedly. "Daddy? Where's Daddy?!" Maddy lifted him into her lap, shushing him by burying his head in her chest.

One of the cemetery workers walked up to the new widow and her sons with a shovel in his hand. He gestured toward Ben with it. "Would you like to place the first shovelful?"

Glancing at Granna, he saw a reassuring nod. The boy stood tall, still sniffling, brushed the tears away with the back of his hand, and took the outstretched handle. He paused over the yawning hole, red roses and brown casket faintly visible, seemingly a mile down, then jammed his shovel into the dirt pile beside him. Ben wanted to cry again, but limited the damage to a quiver of the chin and a face contorted with pain and loss beyond words. He positioned his foot on the shovel blade, put all his weight on it, and scooped up a large mound of dirt.

Tyler twisted around in his mother's lap until they were

almost nose to nose. "I wanna do it! Can I help?" he pleaded, looking back and forth between his mother and brother.

Maddy turned him loose. Ben lowered the handle by way of invitation, and Ty squirmed to the ground, sprinting the few steps to the edge of the grave. Together the two boys emptied the shovel into the chasm, the clods drumming on the casket, scattering and covering the flowers. They leaned toward the grave, watching where the dirt went, to the point where Maddy hopped up and put her arm around Ty's waist so he wouldn't tumble in. She laid her other hand on Ben's back, gave him a reassuring pat, then waited for him to put the shovel down. He seemed not to know what to do, so Maddy put her hand out to take it.

As soon as her fingers closed around the handle, Ben regripped it with both hands and jerked it away with a defiant glare. Then he started shoveling like a madman, attacking the dirt pile and tossing one shovelful after the next toward the grave as fast as he could, sending plumes of earth flying up into the air.

"Honey, stop!" his mother pleaded, but Ben never flagged. Mourners nearby were being showered with dirt. Behind her dark sunglasses, Maddy blushed with embarrassment. "Ben, stop!" she ordered. Another frantic spray of dirt. And another. She reached out and grabbed the handle with both hands and held tight. The two of them gripped the shovel, looking hard into each other's eyes. Seeing the hurt in her firstborn burned right through her. Ben yanked the shovel out of his mother's hands, threw it on the ground, and ran, too young to know he couldn't escape the sadness.

Maddy took a couple of steps after him, but Granna gently held her back. "I'll get him," she said. "Stay," and she took off at a brisk pace. Maddy took Ty by the hand and turned to talk to somebody waiting to offer their condolences.

Ben ran full tilt through the cemetery until he couldn't run another step and collapsed on the thick grass. Shortly Granna came puffing into view. Gasping for breath, she leaned against a tree.

"You wanna give your Granna a heart attack?" she gasped. "You'll be coming to my funeral next!" Ben's ashen expression told her this was the wrong figure of speech for the moment.

"I'm sorry, sweetie, you're right. I shouldn't have said that. But what's wrong with you? You just can't act like that, today of all days. Your father ..."

"My father's dead!" he interrupted, angry and sullen.

Granna sat on the grass with her back against the tree and looked up at the sky. She let out a deep sigh. What could she say? "Look, I know you're hurting, sweetheart. But what you need to do right now is to ask God for answers."

Ben's eyes brimmed with tears. "Like what?" he asked, his voice subdued.

"Pray for God's comfort and protection?"

Ben wasn't buying it. "Remember how you told me God knows everything?" Granna nodded. "Well, did God know my dad was going to die?" She nodded again. Ben's anger started to build, his mind racing. "Why would he let my dad die? And let me and my little brother have to go the rest of our lives without him?"

Granna didn't know what to say. She had no idea in the world why God would let the loving father of these two boys die at the hands of a drunk driver. It was a very good question. As she thought about her answer, she realized that no matter what she said, Ben wouldn't understand. He would have to deal with it in his own way, just as she had had to deal with her own husband's death not long after Ben was born. How could God let a boy grow up without a grandfather, taking her Robert away before he could ever really get to know his grandson? However she answered, it wouldn't make any sense to him. Besides, he was only eleven. How much could he handle?

She took the easy way out. "Ben, there's nothing I can say right now that'll take your pain away. Let's just finish what we came here to do, and I promise you tomorrow we'll talk. Okay?"

Ben nodded and stood up, wiped his face, and held out a hand for her to take. With a mighty grunt, he helped Granna to her feet.

"Careful there, big guy, I wouldn't want you to pull anything!" A hint of a smile played across Ben's face, but it didn't last. Still holding his hand, Granna pulled him toward her and enfolded him in her arms.

"Hey!" They looked around and saw Ty tearing toward them at full speed, with Maddy bringing up the rear. "Granna!" he shouted as he reached their side. "Can we go get ice cream?"

Granna raised a single brow. "Ice cream?" She paused for effect. "Now that sounds like a plan!" She turned to Ben. "How about you, big guy?"

"I guess so," he said without enthusiasm. Granna poked him in the ribs until she finally coaxed out a smile. It wasn't much of one, but it would have to do.

No Experience Necessary

Now what?

That was a question that consumed Maddy's days, one it seemed she and her mother had talked about a hundred times already. A couple of weeks following the funeral, it came up again after the boys went to bed.

The cozy room with its window seat, old-fashioned woodwork, and high ceiling felt cold and empty, drained of the warmth and energy that had always radiated from Patrick wherever he was. Maddy sat on the couch wrapped in a quilt with her mother in a rocker beside her, both of them sipping herbal tea.

"I'm going to have to get a job, Mom," Maddy said, resigned to the fact.

"You can do it, sweetheart," Granna said reassuringly. "You've got a lot to offer some lucky employer."

"Mom, I've never had an employer—need I remind you?" The topic was a sore spot with Maddy. "For crying out loud, I never even finished high school. What am I going to do? Bag groceries?"

"You had more important things to do, like be a mother to that precious boy up there who looks just like his daddy," Granna said, smiling. "It was the only right thing to do—and you know it," she finished, mimicking her daughter.

Once Maddy got pregnant, things happened so fast that the only thing to do was drop out and be a full-time wife and mother. She'd told herself she could never have gone back to Crockett High anyway because she couldn't stand the meanness and teasing of her classmates.

"Okay, you're right," Maddy admitted, "but I promised Patrick I'd finish high school after the baby was born. I never even got a GED."

They sat in silence for a moment. Maddy stared at a spot on the floor and then looked up. "I don't know what to do, Mother," she said. "Thank goodness we had insurance that paid off the house with a little left over. But that won't last long. And after that, I have no earthly idea what to do for money."

"What about getting your real estate license?" Granna suggested, trying her very best not to sound like a nagging mother. Maddy was so fragile these days.

"Oh Mother, please! I don't have the patience, or the desire, to deal with the people and the hours."

The direct approach clearly wouldn't work. She tried another tack. "Well, what have you always wanted to do?"

Maddy glanced at her mother and started to tear up.

"I'm sorry, honey." Strike two. "I know all you ever wanted was to be a good mother and wife, and you are."

Granna stopped rocking and looked intently at her daughter. "I'll tell you what. Would it make things easier if I put my busy life on hold and move in with you for a while? To help with the boys until you get things together?"

Maddy stopped crying, staring at her mother in curious disbelief. "Your busy life? Are you kidding me? You haven't done a thing since Daddy died!"

"Well," Granna said flatly, "it's a hard life trying to look forty when you're almost sixty." Mother and daughter stared at each other, then burst out laughing. It felt so good to laugh again.

"Seriously, Mom," Maddy said after she caught her breath, "you'd do that? Move in?"

Granna gave her the stern I'm-your-mother-and-don't-you-forget-it look Maddy had seen all her life. "Do I look like I'm kidding, young lady?" They laughed again. "Seriously, honey, I'd do anything for you. You know that."

Sniffling, Maddy leaned into her for a little-girl hug. "Will you go get me a job?"

It wasn't her typical 6:00 a.m. response to the noxious buzz of the alarm. This Sunday morning, Maddy jumped out of bed like a woman with a plan. Throwing on an old sweat suit and pulling her long blonde hair into a ponytail, she trotted downstairs to the kitchen, where her mother sat at the table drinking coffee and working yesterday's crossword puzzle.

"We going to church this morning?" Granna asked.

Maddy heaved a sigh that said, "Oh, Mother!" so she wouldn't have to.

"I'm telling you," Granna went on, "it's been two weeks without worshiping your Lord." She paused, choosing her words carefully, trying not to sound bossy. "It makes all the difference in the world to me when I've got a lot on my mind."

Maddy knew she was right, which made her advice all the more irritating. She felt the need to get her spiritual life back on track, but she was so tired and scattered. The whole notion that Patrick could be taken by God on purpose had planted a stubborn seed of doubt deep inside her. Besides, her mother could be so bossy sometimes!

"Mother, when I want your opinion, I'll ask for it," she said curtly.

"I was just saying ..."

"You don't need to say anything. I'm almost twenty-seven. When are you going to start treating me like an adult?"

Granna shrugged. "Probably never. How about fetching today's crossword puzzle for your ol' momma? I'm about done with this one."

Maddy filled her coffee cup, opened the front door, and made a brisk beeline for the morning paper on the sidewalk. She would have gone out for it first thing even if her mother hadn't asked. Back inside, she pulled the classifieds from the center of the paper and tossed the rest on the table in front of her mother as she headed out the back.

There, Maddy settled into her little corner of paradise. Patrick had laid out a beautiful garden just for her — a sanctuary, a place to escape to when the kids got to be too much or she needed a quiet place to think. Something was in bloom almost year-round, including all of her favorites: daffodils, tulips, daisies, roses, orchids, periwinkles. And he'd worked like a dog to keep it looking perfect for her. She felt so close to him there even now. Everywhere she looked, her eye fell on a shrub he'd planted or a border he'd trimmed. It was almost like he'd come in just ahead of her to tidy things up. In the center of the garden, Patrick had built a small arbor with a swing so she could sit and enjoy its peacefulness.

She swung gently back and forth as she scanned the classifieds, crossing out every job that required experience. That didn't leave many. But it did leave a listing she circled under "Restaurants" that read:

Wanted Immediately
Waitress needed in a small but
busy family restaurant. No experience
necessary, will train. $5.13 per hour
plus tips. Applications available online.
Bring applications to Shuckley's
Restaurant, 1215 Old Tampa Hwy.

"No experience necessary," she said to herself. "Yup, that's me."

The morning breeze stirred the trees and rustled the flowers of her backyard oasis, but the peacefulness of the setting was a world away from the turmoil she felt festering inside. "What has happened to my life?" she wondered aloud. Where was God in all this?

"What's going on, Lord? You gave me everything I ever dreamed of. A strong, handsome, faithful, loving husband who took care of me and protected me. Two precious, carefree boys. A rock-solid faith in you that I knew could carry me through anything. And now what? Now I'm a high school dropout single mom with two kids, looking for a minimum wage job. A widow." A *widow.* The word gave her cold shivers.

What did God think he was doing?

The longer she sat, the madder she got. "What is it you want me to learn, Father?" she demanded. "Was I too content?" Anger and frustration and sadness swirled around inside her, roiling up like some toxic stew. "Is that it? Did I not pay you enough attention?" Her voice got louder. "Why, God? Why? Why!"

Granna heard the shouting and walked to the edge of the kitchen stoop. "Maddy?"

Maddy looked up. "It's okay," she said. "I'm all right. I just lost it for a minute."

Granna took a step off the porch. Maddy held out her arms, and her mother ran to embrace her. The two sat in the swing for a long moment, rocking gently, holding each other.

Granna noticed the marked-up classifieds. "Job hunting?"

Maddy nodded.

"Any nibbles?"

Maddy pointed at the restaurant listing. "Here's all you can do without experience."

"Great! When do you start?"

Maddy was confused. She shook the cobwebs out. "Wait a minute. What?"

"When do you start?"

"Mother, I haven't applied for it yet."

"Well, what are you waiting for? Somebody to call you up and offer it to you? Get hopping." She gave her a playful push out of the swing and a swat on the rear.

Maddy stood by the swing with her head down. "A waitress in a diner?" she asked in a small, ashamed voice.

"I remember my first job," Granna said breezily.

Maddy eyed her, incredulous. "*You*? Mom, you never worked a day in your life, and you know it!"

"*Au contraire*, my dear, but I did. No reason for you to remember it because you were only two. Your father was laid off from his job at the factory for six months, and who do you suppose came to the rescue?"

"Not *you*." It was half question, half statement.

"Yes, me. And I'll have you know I was the best waitress Shuckley's has ever seen before or since."

Maddy's eyes widened. "You've got to be kidding. Shuckley's? They've been here all this time?"

"And still serve what is arguably the best meatloaf on the planet. And let me tell you something else, little missy. Don't you hang your head around me for waiting tables. There's no shame in working in a restaurant—or anywhere else—when you have mouths to feed. Your father and Patrick both always said to stand tall and be proud of what you do. Was Patrick too proud to push a broom at night?" Maddy shook her head. "You're darn right he wasn't, especially come payday. Honey, pride is the devil setting you up for humiliation, but humiliation is preparing you to be humble."

Revived, inspired, and encouraged, Maddy gave her mother a peck on the cheek and walked quickly toward the kitchen door.

"Where are you headed in such a rush?"

"To the computer to fill out an application," she said, throwing the words over her shoulder. "I'm gonna be the best waitress they've ever seen!" Before the door could close behind her, she popped her head back out. "By the way, do you mind staying with the boys tomorrow morning? I'm going to check on the application in person."

"Are you kidding?" Granna scowled. "Those monsters?" She broke into a beaming Granna grin. "Go on, get that application form done. I'm gonna roust them out of the sack and take them to church."

"Great! Love you! See you around lunch time!"

Walking through the door at Shuckley's Restaurant was a journey back in time. Booths lined the big plate glass windows looking out onto the sidewalk, their red plastic upholstery with glittery gold streaks matching the stools at the counter. The old jukebox had been replaced with one that played CDs but looked about the same on the outside. The air smelled of coffee and cooking grease. Laminated menus were updated between printings with little pieces of masking tape that covered old prices with new ones, and the daily special inserts were produced on what was no doubt the last functioning manual typewriter in south Florida.

It was easy to see who was in charge. Late middle-aged and comfortably padded, Lizzie wore a crisp blue skirt, white blouse, and one of those little nurse-like caps worn by waitresses in old movies, anchored to her luxuriant red hair with a dozen bobby pins. She was just finishing a phone call when an attractive, slightly bewildered-looking young woman with a long dark blonde ponytail stepped inside and stood near the door.

"One, sweetie?" she asked, snapping her chewing gum with seasoned panache.

"Uh, no," Maddy replied hesitantly. "I'm actually, uh, wanting to apply for the job you posted in the paper yesterday. I sent in an application online."

"Come back in an hour, after the breakfast crowd, and we'll talk," the waitress said, and walked away.

Maddy stood with a blank stare on her face. *Come back? Humf!* Snubbed by a country diner! This whole job thing was going to be impossible. *Maybe I should just forget about it.* Since she couldn't think of anything better to do, she went back out to the van and waited.

An hour later, the waitress met her in the doorway. She wiped her hand on a dishtowel and stuck it out. "Lizzie," she said.

"Maddy Doherty," Maddy said with a nervous smile.

"You came back. You must really need the job."

"Actually, I do."

Lizzie smiled. She could size up new hires pretty quickly, and this girl was a winner. "Have a seat at the counter and fill out this schedule sheet saying when you're available, or you can take it home and bring it back later."

Maddy was seated and writing before Lizzie finished her sentence. When she finished, Maddy stood and waited for Lizzie to come by again. The waitress looked over to see Maddy get up. "Now, you didn't go and change your mind did you?" she said in a voice that carried easily over the clatter and chatter from one end of the room to the other.

"No, of course not," Maddy called back, smiling. Lizzie took the sheet and scanned down it quickly.

"I haven't worked before because I've been a mom at home," Maddy explained. "We had kids right away, and my husband and I thought it was important for me to stay home and be with them." She looked earnestly at Lizzie.

"You look like her, you know."

"Beg pardon?"

"You are Olivia Alexander's daughter, aren't you?"

Maddy realized her mouth was hanging open. "Um, yes, ma'am, that's my mother all right. Do you know her?"

"Know her?" Lizzie chuckled. "When you walked in here an hour ago with that nervous, wide-eyed look on your face, you could have been her coming through the same door twenty-five years ago. Carl and I had just taken over this place from his dad.

Your father was laid off at the plant, and your mother made it her business to take up the slack until he got called back." Maddy was speechless. The story was true after all. "So, to change the subject, when would you like to start?"

Maddy looked puzzled. "You mean, I have the job?"

"It's yours if you want it, sugar. I don't see a herd of hopefuls beating down my door asking for the gig, do you?"

"Well," Maddy admitted, "I guess not."

"Welcome to Shuckley's." The two shook hands again, Maddy beaming with a sense of mission accomplished.

On her drive home, Maddy played the Shuckley's scenario over in her head. Had her mother had a hand in what just went on? If not, this job search business was not nearly as hard as it was supposed to be. Any other time in her life, she'd have said it could be God at work, but she wasn't so sure about that right now. Regardless of how it had happened, she was delighted.

Granna and the boys were waiting for her in the living room.

"Well . . . ?" her mother asked, perched on the edge of her seat.

"Well what?" Maddy asked, playing the game until her joy gave her away. "I got the job!" she screamed, fists in the air in triumph. Then they were all screaming, jumping around in celebration. As the noise died down, Maddy took her mother's arm.

"Mom, now tell the truth. Did you have anything to do with me getting this job?"

Granna looked straight at her, expressionless. "I don't know what on earth you're talking about." Then louder, "Who's ready for lunch?"

"Me!" screamed Ty, leaping from the sofa and following her into the kitchen. "I wanna help."

"Sure you can, sweetheart," Granna answered. Maddy mouthed the words "thank you" to her mother, who gave her a "you're welcome" wink in return.

The New Normal

After three months of dishing up legendary meatloaf, Maddy could see that, even with tips, her tiny paycheck from Shuckley's wasn't going to keep them afloat for long. Bills were starting to back up, and she carefully hoarded what insurance money there was left, using it only when she had no alternative and scrimping as much as she could. Besides making more money, she wanted a job that gave her a sense of satisfaction and accomplishment — a career for the long term. Lizzie was a waitress, but she was also a business owner. What should she do?

One night after another double shift, Maddy trooped slowly up the stairs to her room. The kids had been in bed for an hour and her mom was probably asleep too by now. Still in her uniform, she flopped down across the bed and kicked off her shoes. There was a soft knock at the bedroom door. Granna peeked in.

"You awake?"

"Yeah, but not for long," Maddy said, rolling over and sitting on the side of the bed.

"How ya doing?"

No answer.

"What's the matter, honey?"

Maddy fell back on the bed and stared up at the ceiling. "I don't know, Mom. One day it's thinking about Patrick, another day it's thinking about that drunk who hit him. Is he just skipping merrily through life without a clue as to how he devastated us? I get so mad sometimes, and I'm not sure if I'm mad at God or at that drunk. I can't stop thinking about it."

Her mother sat beside her, stroking her forehead.

"Mom, how did you feel when Daddy died?"

A distant look came into Granna's eyes. "Alone. Afraid. Mad."

Maddy could see she had touched a spot that was still tender. "I'm sorry, Mom. We just never talked about it." They hugged each other tightly.

"Our husbands were good men who left us wonderful memories, wonderful legacies," Granna said. The two of them sat close on the bed holding hands, their shoulders touching. "And you've got the special blessing of Patrick's letters to God."

"I know, Mom."

"I love it when you read them to the boys. It gives them a chance to know their father like most boys in their situation never would. And that old Bible of his—what a treasure!"

"He was a scribbler, all right," Maddy affirmed. "Honestly, I like reading Patrick's notes almost as much as reading the Scripture. It makes me feel so close to him."

"Where did you put all that stuff?"

"The letters are in boxes with the rest of Patrick's things I wanted to keep. His Bible's still in the bedside table."

Maddy sighed and brushed a stray strand of hair out of her face.

"Tired, huh?" Granna asked.

"Absolutely bushed," Maddy admitted. "I'm glad to have any kind of job under the circumstances, but I feel like I should do something more than wait tables in an old country diner for the rest of my life." They lay back on the bed dangling their feet over the edge, clutching pillows to themselves like three-year-olds holding their favorite stuffed toys.

Granna broke the silence. "What did you want to be when you were growing up?"

Maddy furrowed her brow and really thought about it. "An actress," she decided finally.

"Well, I think that's off the table. Nothing else?"

Maddy thought some more. "I did think about becoming a doctor."

Granna raised her eyebrows in surprise. "Really? I never knew that."

"I'm still full of surprises." Another pause.

"Maddy, have you ever thought about being a nurse?"

Maddy turned to look at her. "Do you think I could do that?" The hint of excitement in her voice told her mother she'd hit on something.

"Are you kidding? You can be anything you want to be. I know it."

Maddy scrunched up her nose. "But I didn't even finish high school."

"I'll alert the media," Granna said on her way out the door.

Still in her work clothes, Maddy turned off the bedside lamp and stared out at the full moon shining in through the blinds.

She was so tired she couldn't even think. Where was God these days? Didn't he see that growing stack of bills in the kitchen? Didn't he know how her feet were killing her at the end of these endless double shifts? "If you're so smart and know so much, what should I do, God?" she wondered aloud, eyes fixed on the moon. "I'm really stuck this time. What do you want me to do with my life? I am so worn out at the end of the day I can hardly lift another coffee pot, much less be a mother to two frightened and lonesome boys. I'm broke, I'm scared to death, and I don't know why all this has happened. Will I ever know?"

Was God listening? *Maybe the answer isn't to ask for reasons why. Maybe I shouldn't be praying for all my problems to go away, but for strength and wisdom and faith to face those problems.* "I used to be so sure you knew my needs before I even asked," she prayed. "I want to be sure now. You know what we have in the bank. You know what's in my boys' hearts better than I do. Please, God, give me strength. Give me faith to trust in you...."

The overhead light clicked on, temporarily blinding her and stopping her in midsentence. Her mother walked over to the bed and thrust a sheaf of papers at her.

"Here!"

"What's this?" Maddy asked, squinting up.

"Everything you need to know to become a nurse. I just got it off the Internet."

Maddy rifled through the pages excitedly, looking at GED study guides and descriptions of nursing programs in Orlando. Chuckling softly, she put the pages down on the bedside table, got up to turn off the overhead light, and lay back down on the bed.

"Is this your answer, Lord?" She smiled up at the moon and stars through the window. "Maybe things are going to be okay."

It took four years. Four years working every shift she could snag at Shuckley's. Four years of nursing school while her mother took care of Ben and Ty. Four years of not enough sleep, not enough time with the boys, not enough time for herself. Now at long last it was graduation day. What had once seemed impossible was a done deal. Sitting in her cap and gown with the other graduates, she turned around to wave at her family in the crowd. Tyler was seven now and had grown into quite a handsome little soccer player. Ben was fifteen, feisty, long-haired, hooked on rock 'n' roll, and had an inscrutable combination of genuine charm and annoying teen attitude.

Maddy gave her crew a little wave. Granna held two enthusiastic thumbs up. Ty waved wildly with both hands. Ben, boredom oozing from every pore, flipped his hair and turned away. Her mother had been her rock, had made it possible for her to get through this. She had thrown everything into taking care of the boys, cooking for them, herding them to school, soccer practice, and band camp, and dealing with Ben's cynicism. Ty scarcely remembered his father, but his older brother still felt the pain of his absence.

"Madalynn Doherty."

At the sound of her name she stood and crossed the stage to accept her diploma. Life had been especially hard for her these long years without Patrick, stretching herself so thin between getting by in the present and planning for the future. She took her precious roll of parchment from the dean, shook her hand, and walked off the other side of the stage. Eying her little cheering section as she took her seat, she caught Ben smiling in spite of himself.

Maddy began her career on the maternity ward at Memorial Medical Center, working the midnight shift, which paid a little more than the regular day schedule. Nursing for Maddy was everything she'd ever hoped it would be. Seeing other mothers bringing new life into the world reminded her of all the ecstatic feelings when she'd had her own children—without the pain, the tension, or the epidural. She especially loved being in Labor and Delivery for a couple's first child. Patrick had so loved that unforgettable shared moment in their lives together. Watching other fathers, she could see Patrick's face full of pride and tears as clearly as if he were standing in the room with them.

Maddy worked three twelve-hour shifts a week, which earned her a full week's pay yet gave her four days with her family. It was time to get back into her children's lives in a way that had been impossible while she was waitressing and in school. Also, she had a chance to rebuild her own life after burning the candle at both ends for so long, to start restoring what the past four years had drained out of her.

She had been nervous her first night. Any job must be confusing in the beginning, but this was special. Helpless babies and their mothers were depending on her. It was exciting but nerve-wracking at the same time.

She'd been told to report to the nurses' station on the fourth floor. Stepping off the elevator, she heard a booming voice ahead of her. It wasn't loud, just big, though no doubt it could be plenty loud whenever the need arose. As she came around the corner, Maddy saw that the owner of the voice was big too. Everything about her was larger than life—big-boned, big-featured, big-haired, her black skin contrasting with a mountain of luxuriant gold dreadlocks. Yet as Maddy would soon learn, the biggest thing about her was her heart. The woman was dressed in a nurse's uniform and stood behind the counter at the nurses' station with a clipboard in her hand, a big hand that made the clipboard look like a toy.

Looking up, the woman saw Maddy and their eyes met. The woman smiled a dazzling smile.

"Honey, you must be Madalynn Doherty!"

Startled, Maddy slowed a little but kept walking. "Yes. People call me Maddy—"

"Well, Maddy, welcome to the maternity floor at Memorial Medical Center. My name's Carol, and I'll be your hostess this evening. Table for one?"

Maddy cocked an eyebrow. "Excuse me?"

"Honey, I'm just funnin' with you a little. Been known to do that from time to time." When she chuckled she made a low, friendly sort of growl. "My name's Carol Martin. I'm the shift supervisor because nobody else would have the job!" She put down the clipboard and held out both her hands. "Welcome." Maddy took them, strong, rough, yet tender hands.

"Thanks. I know I've got a lot to learn."

"Right you are, honey, and we're going to start with the three most important things this minute: where's the bathroom? where's the coffee? and where's the pencil sharpener?"

Maddy could feel her unease slipping away as Carol showed her where to put her things and started explaining the routine. Over the course of the shift, she introduced her to her patients, the rest of the nurses, and anybody else who happened by at that time of night.

During her meal break in the wee hours of the morning, Carol came into the staff lounge with a young nurse Maddy hadn't seen yet.

"Honey, meet Jamie Lynn Byrnes. She's one of us. Been helping out on another floor this evening and has now rejoined the A-team. Now if you'll excuse me, somewhere there's a bedpan calling my name." Carol breezed out the door as quickly as she'd entered.

"Hi, Maddy. Pleased to meet you," Jamie Lynn said. She had a strong Old South accent that Maddy liked listening to.

"Thanks, Jamie."

"Jamie Lynn. It's one of those Southern 'twofer' names—two for the price of one."

"Sorry. Jamie Lynn." They both smiled. "Would you like to join me?"

"Sure." Jamie Lynn sat down at the table, opened a plastic container of homemade chicken salad, and started to eat. Jamie Lynn was a few years younger than she was, Maddy decided. Her dark brown hair was pulled into a twist on top of her head. The gray eyes looked kind, but Maddy thought she saw sadness in them.

"Everybody has sure gone out of their way to make me feel welcome," Maddy said, "especially Carol."

"Isn't she a piece of work?" Jamie Lynn answered. "She treated me so nice when I first started."

"How long have you been here?"

"Two years. Before that I was a waitress in Tupelo, but I couldn't make a living at it. Besides, I didn't like getting pinched."

"That sounds like me," Maddy said, suddenly animated. "Not the pinching part, but I was a waitress too. My husband died in a car accident, and I had to take care of my boys."

"How many kids?"

"Two. Ben's fifteen and Tyler's seven."

"My boy just turned four. John Joseph Byrnes. His daddy was killed in Iraq."

"Oh, Jamie Lynn, I'm so sorry."

"Thanks. Sounds like you and I are going to have plenty to talk about over our leftovers."

At eight o'clock on Saturday morning, Ty came barreling into his mother's bedroom. She'd been home from her shift for less than an hour.

"Mom!"

Maddy sat bolt upright in bed, tired, confused, disoriented. "What? What is it?"

Ty flitted to the window and pulled down the blanket Maddy had put up to block out the sun so she could sleep during the day. He was in his soccer uniform and had a ball under his arm.

"It is that time already?" Maddy asked with a weary yawn, though she already knew the answer.

"Uh huh. And I'm gonna be late if we don't get going!"

Maddy rolled over and pulled the pillow over her head with a muffled groan.

Still at the window, Ty twisted open the blinds and let the full morning sun stream in.

"Ty!" came the muted cry from under the pillow.

"What, Mom? I can't hear you! More, you said?"

His mother groaned again. "You're gonna pay for this, little man. Mark my words—You. Will. Pay." Tyler stood giggling at the window as Maddy threw back the covers, sprang from the bed, and charged.

Ty bounded across the bed, cleats and all, and out the door. "You'll have to catch me first!" he taunted, his voice fading as he ran down the stairs.

Maddy sat on the edge of her bed, smoothing out the cleat prints in the sheet and gathering herself. "This thirty-minute night's sleep is for the birds," she said to no one in particular as she dragged herself toward the bathroom.

Running into the kitchen, Ty found Granna standing over the stove, making pancakes.

"Wow, are we in a hurry this morning?" she asked.

"I have a game in a few minutes, Granna! You coming?"

She flashed him her big patented Granna smile. "Wouldn't miss it for the world."

Tyler pulled a carton of orange juice from the fridge and poured himself a glass.

"You hungry?" Granna asked, scooping up another pancake with the spatula.

"No ma'am." Tyler shook his head. "I got up early and ate some cereal. Coach Dave says not to eat anything heavy before a game. I might puke."

"I wish you wouldn't use words like that, Ty," Granna said with grandmotherly disapproval.

"What? *Puke*?" he asked, the picture of innocence. "Well, that's what he said."

"But he didn't say it in the kitchen at breakfast time."

"Geez, do you guys have to be so loud?" It was Ben, shuffling into the kitchen, plugged, as usual, into his iPod.

"Well, good morning, sleepyhead," said Granna cheerfully.

Ben shrugged her off, sat down at the table, and pulled out one earbud. "It is Saturday, you know. Supposed to be the one day we can bag in."

"But I've got a game!" Ty announced.

"And that means I gotta go to it?" Ben grumped. "Now? You should see all the Zs I left on the pillow."

"We're gonna cream them!" Ty declared, his enthusiasm undampened. "You wait and see!"

Wordlessly, Ben made his move toward the stack of pancakes, nodding to the sound of the music only he could hear.

Roller Coaster

Ty looked forward to Saturday soccer games. He had loved kicking the soccer ball around in the yard with his dad, but that was more than half his life ago. The memory of those days had faded to an indistinct mist of recollections that the games helped keep alive.

This brisk Saturday morning at the playing field, Ty was brimming with confidence, ready to do battle and give whatever it took to win. "I'm gonna score five goals today!" he boasted as he walked toward the warm-up area beside Colt Turner, a stocky, good-natured boy who was one of the team's best fullbacks.

"Five? Is that all?" Colt goaded playfully.

In reply, Ty gave his ball a furious kick, blasting it into the back of the nearest goal net. Colt trotted off to retrieve it and kick it back. John Edwin, a tall black boy and one of their best tacklers, trotted toward the field with them.

Samantha Perryfield came jogging in from the parking lot. "Hey, Sam," Tyler said, waving. Sam lived five houses down the street from Ty, and the two had known each other all their lives. Since they were the same age, they were in the same grade in school, and now they were on the same soccer team too. Sam was one of Ty's very best friends, even if she was a girl. She wasn't chicken or gossipy, like girls tended to be sometimes, but was far more like a normal person. She and Ty were about the same size, and Sam was a good runner, a good midfielder. Today her auburn hair was pulled back with a rubber band.

"Hey, Ty," she said. "What's up?"

"We're gonna cream the Harpeth Hornets, that's what!"

"Awesome!"

"All right, you buggers, gather round for warm-ups." Coach Dave Underhill's unmistakable English accent carried across the field, summoning Ty and his friends to pre-game drills. Dave loved soccer as much as Ty did and Patrick had. When he just missed making the British national team, he came to the US, where his passion for the game—not to mention his accent—soon gave him a choice of coaching jobs. The work with the West Side Tornadoes was something he did just for the fun of it, planting a love for soccer in a culture where other sports had a big head start.

The team formed a circle. They were seven and eight years old, full of energy, just getting coordinated enough to execute basic moves reasonably well. "Let's go, step-ups!" Dave yelled. The kids put one foot onto a ball, then the other, alternating back and forth. Seriousness mixed with a seven-year-old's silliness got the best of Tyler, who started to giggle. "Ty!" Coach Dave called sternly. "Why don't you lead the team in a trot around the pitch?"

Ty darted off, trotting backward until the others fell in line, complaining pitifully like they did every week. "Suck it up, you bunch of babies!" he piped, mimicking what he heard Coach Dave say sometimes and triggering another round of good-natured moans and groans.

Catching his breath after his run, hands on his hips, Ty

walked up to Coach Dave as the rest of the team jogged and straggled in behind him. "Where do you want me today, Coach?"

"I'll start you at midfield," he said.

"Captains!" yelled the referee as he motioned for the team captains to join him in the middle of the field. Tyler and John ran to the center circle and joined the captains from the Hornets. John called the toss.

"Tails!"

Tails it was. "We want the ball!" Ty snapped decisively, then backpedaled toward the sideline.

Coach Dave started the pre-game chatter: "Okay, let's go! All offense, attack the goal and follow through. If they're playing with your ball, take it away! The best defense wins, right?"

"Nope, the team with the most goals wins!" said Ty, full of seven-year-old fight. His teammates voiced their approval.

"Okay, smart alec," said the coach, "then you better score the most goals!" That pumped everybody up even more. They circled around, put their hands on top of each other's, and chanted, "Go, Tornadoes, go!" then broke the circle with a battle cry as the starters ran to their positions.

Tornadoes were in royal blue, Hornets in yellow. The starting whistle blew. Colt rolled the ball out in front of Ty, who dribbled fast toward the goal with little resistance. Near the net, a Hornet fullback waited. "Bring it on!" the bigger boy growled as Ty approached. Charging toward his opponent, Ty made a quick pass to Colt, who took two steps then sent a rifle shot toward the net. The goalie dived for a save but he was too late. The ball flew into the upper right corner.

"Yeah!" Ty shouted as he and Colt exchanged high fives.

That first goal set the tone for the morning's game. The

Tornadoes dominated the field, and by the time the final whistle sounded they had won six to one, with Ty making three of the goals, two of them unassisted.

The teams lined up to shake hands. Walking down the line with his hand out ("good game, good game, good game"), Ty suddenly felt a searing pain in his head. He stumbled and bent over, holding his forehead with both palms. Maddy, standing on the sideline talking with Granna, saw Ty stop and grab his head, but he straightened up almost right away and went on through the handshake line. He seemed all right.

Ty went to the bench to grab his gear. Coach Dave intercepted him and gave him a pat on the back. "That sort of play will get you to the championship, mate. Well played."

Ty waved his thanks and headed for his family.

"Honey—," Maddy began.

"I'm fine, Mom," Ty said without looking up. "I just have a headache."

"Geez, runt," Ben interjected, "you knock your brain loose with that last goal?"

"Maybe I did," Ty answered with a wan smile. Granna wrapped an arm around him as they headed to the van. "I just need to lay down."

By the time they got home, Ty was fast asleep. Ben jumped out, grabbed his skateboard, and headed down the sidewalk.

"You'll be home for supper?" Maddy yelled after him as she reached over to wake Ty.

"Yep," Ben yelled back.

Maddy gently roused Ty and helped him undo his seatbelt. "Does your head still hurt?" she asked.

"It's a little better."

He was too big to let her carry him, even if she could have.

She put her hands under his arms and helped him into the house and up the stairs to his room, which was packed with sports memorabilia, posters, and souvenirs, soccer stuff in particular. Trophies lined the shelves, and on the wall over his bed was the best thing of all—a number ten Los Angeles Galaxy jersey autographed by Landon Donovan, all-time leader in scoring and assists on the US national team. On the nightstand next to his bed was a photo of a younger Tyler with Ben, Mom, and Dad.

Ty sat on the edge of his bed, looking at the picture. He kissed his hand and touched it to the glass as he lay down.

"He'd be really proud of you today, you know," his mother said.

"Yeah, I know." He settled himself in bed, still looking at the photograph.

His mother left for a minute and came back with a dose of children's pain medication and a glass of water. "Here, this ought to help." As he sat up to take the pills, she leaned down and kissed him on his forehead. "You get some rest, now. If you need anything more, just holler."

"I will." He closed his eyes as she backed out of the room.

Closing the door and heading for the stairs, she met Granna coming up.

"He's okay, isn't he?"

"I don't know, Mother. I hope so."

"Of course he's okay my dear. You worry too much."

Maddy answered with a deep sigh as they went down the stairs together. "Mom, have you noticed him with any headaches before?"

Granna thought hard. "I can only remember one or two maybe. Why?"

They walked into the kitchen. Maddy sat at the table as

Granna started a pot of coffee. "What is it, dear?" Granna insisted. "What's bothering you?"

Maddy nervously ran her hands through her hair. "He's had a lot of headaches over the last few months. It's not normal for a seven-year-old to have so many. And they don't seem to be caused by anything. They just crop up out of nowhere."

Granna looked up from the coffee pot. "So, what is it that you're worried about?"

"I'm not sure," Maddy answered with a note of frustration. "But when you take him to his check-up in a couple weeks, make sure and mention it. Have them see if it's … anything serious."

Granna pulled a chair out and sat beside her. "Sweetheart, why on earth would you think a few headaches mean anything serious? People get headaches all the time."

Maddy considered the point. Maybe she was being paranoid about the whole thing. But a feeling she couldn't quite describe kept nagging at her. "I'm not sure. Intuition, maybe. But would you ask, just for my sake?"

Granna stood to finish making their coffee. "I think you're being a bit of a worrywart," she said with a hint of a chuckle, "but okay, I promise."

They were deciding what to make for lunch when the mailbox on the porch creaked open. "There's Walter," Granna announced.

Walter Finley had been their mailman ever since they moved to the house on Laurel Lane. It would be hard to imagine a friendlier person. Walter obviously loved his work and enjoyed the people he met. He'd known some of them the entire ten years he'd been on this route. There was the Perryfield house, where old Grandpa Perryfield waited impatiently for his mail every day. And there was Erin Miller, *Miss* Erin Miller, who loved her flowers and had the most incredible plant beds imaginable every season of the year. She was actually a little smitten with Walter Finley. Not that he was anything special to look at. He was probably between forty-five and fifty, with salt-and-pepper hair and unremarkable features. Maybe it was the uniform; all the single ladies on the route looked forward to the sight of Mr. Finley coming up the walk. And that included Granna.

Ben and Ty swore he was her boyfriend. "I'm too old for boyfriends," she'd say, trying to be stern. But then she'd wipe her hands on her apron and hightail it to the porch to talk to him.

"Hi, Walter," Granna said, opening the door.

"Hey, Mrs. Alexander. Can't beat a day like this, can you?"

"It is nice." He took the outgoing mail from the box, handed her what he had, and turned to leave. "Did you change your route today?" she asked.

Walter stopped and thought a second. "No, I don't believe so."

"I thought you were a little earlier than usual."

"Must be the anticipation of my charming face. Makes it seem sooner," he kidded.

"Oh, Walter, you're a mess! Would you like a glass of water or anything?"

"Thanks, but no. Better keep rolling along here."

"Okay. Guess I'll see you Monday."

Standing in the doorway, she noticed Maddy watching her intently. "Oh, my goodness," she declared pointedly, looking down her nose. "Aren't we a bunch of nosey-Roseys!"

Dressed in her usual blue scrubs and running her usual ten minutes late, Maddy raced down the hall past the photo of

Patrick and herself, which she walked by a dozen times a day. Hurried as she was, she stopped long enough to look into his eyes and remember what wonderful, content, carefree days those had been. They seemed a lifetime ago.

"I didn't know it would be so hard," she whispered to him with a melancholy smile.

Bounding down the stairs, she came into the kitchen, where her mother stood at the sink, scrubbing a pan.

"Hey, Mom, can you ..."

Both hands in the sudsy water, Granna looked up with a smile and gestured with her head. "Sweetie, they're already in the oven. Been there almost an hour. I must be a pretty bad cook if you can't smell your favorite dish."

Maddy opened the fridge and took out an apple and a ginger ale. "I'm just in a hurry, Mom. Woke up too late." She kissed her mother on the cheek.

Granna glanced at the fruit and soft drink. "At least you'll have a healthy dinner."

"I'll grab something later." Maddy headed out the kitchen door.

"You're going to church with us in the morning, right?" Granna called after her.

Maddy was busy, she was late, she wasn't thinking about tomorrow, she wasn't sure what she thought about church these days. She took a deep breath.

"I don't know, Mom. I guess I should, shouldn't I?"

Wiping her hands with a dishtowel, Olivia nodded. "Face it, he misses you."

Maddy put one hand on her hip and glanced at the clock on the kitchen wall. "Okay, I'll bite. Who misses me?"

"Why, God, of course," Granna announced, all innocence, but with a devious smile.

"I'll think about it," Maddy said, closing the door behind her.

Driving to work, she thought about her mother's less-than-subtle suggestion. *It has been a while.* She knew deep down that she used her hectic schedule as a single working mother as an excuse. She could get to church more often if she really wanted to, but she found herself wavering sometimes.

As much as she loved God, the big question still rose up in her heart when she least expected it, blocking out the sun: Why? Why, why, why did Patrick have to die? Since that had happened, she'd been on a sort of spiritual roller coaster and wasn't sure how to get off. Sometimes it all seemed fairly clear, but then the anger and sadness would come roaring back, and when they did, all those dark doubts came with them.

Going to church would bring her closer to the answer. And it sure wouldn't hurt Ben. The older he got, the more distant and cynical he became. Maybe a regular dose of church was exactly what he needed.

She worried about Ben. Perhaps it had been a mistake for her to start nursing school so soon after Patrick died. Ben needed her more than she realized, and she wasn't there for him. Ben took his father's death harder than Ty, both then and now. If only she could have reached up and stopped the sun, stopped time in its tracks while she finished school so she could have been with them more! Before she knew it, Ben would be off to college. *That's when he'll appreciate all I've done.* Ty was still young enough for her to get a handle on before it was too late. In some ways, the boys were polar opposites. Tyler was more loving and caring, and way too much of a momma's boy ever to give her the kind of worry Ben did.

Coming to herself, Maddy shook her head with a start and realized in disbelief that she was still parked in her own driveway. Genuinely panicked now at the time, she threw the van in gear and headed for the hospital as fast as the law allowed. Maybe a little faster.

Treasure

Ty sailed down the stairs and into the kitchen. "Mom?" he called out.

"You just missed her, sweetie," Granna told him. "What do you need?"

"I just wanted to tell her good-bye!" He ran out the door and into the yard, yelling and waving at the van as it turned the corner at the end of the street. Heading back inside he heard a familiar voice call his name.

"Hey, Ty!" It was Sam.

"Sam—hey, how's it going?"

Sam came up the sidewalk from her house to the Dohertys'. Her hair streamed out behind her as she ran, her eyes sparkling in the sunlight. Sam didn't have any brothers or sisters. It was just her and her parents, Tom and Liz, and her grandfather. Now there was a character. In fact, Grandpa Perryfield was a whole trunk full of characters because he'd been an actor, and a little bit of every role seemed to have rubbed off on him. He had a wonderful, rich, deep voice that he could make sound like practically anybody, and he always wore very elegant, very old clothes, even on Saturday. At times he came off pretty grumpy. Sam said he hadn't always been that way, but since her grandmother died and he moved in with them, he got that way once in a while. Taking everything into account, Ty thought Mr. Perryfield was a pretty neat guy. And Sam was tops, as good a friend as any boy could be.

"You played a great game," Sam said.

"Thanks," Ty answered. "You had some big saves out there too. Yeah, we stung the Hornets big-time! Hey, wanna play checkers?"

Sam's grandpa had taught her how to play, then she had taught Ty, and by now they were an even match. Whenever they got together, they usually played a game or two. Because they were at the same skill level, games could take a long time.

"Sure, let's play," Sam answered as they walked inside.

The kitchen smelled wonderful. "Mmmmm, what's for supper?" Sam asked.

"Well, I'm glad somebody finally noticed!" Granna said. "Hi, Sam. It's roasted pork tenderloin. I bet there's enough for an extra mouth. Want to join us?"

"I'll say," Sam answered happily. "My parents are going out tonight, and Grandpa said he'd heat up some chicken potpies. Pork roast sounds great."

"All right. I'll give your granddad a call."

"Thanks!"

"Don't you two stray too far. We're gonna eat soon."

The kids climbed the stairs to Ty's room and set up the checkerboard on the floor.

"Is your mom at work?" Sam wondered as they started the game.

"Yeah, she works three nights a week. Then she comes home wiped out. I had to blast her out of bed this morning to make it to the game." A new thought came to him. "Hey, you wanna see a video of me playing?"

Sam liked soccer and other sports, but not nearly as much as

Ty. Yet that's what friends were for—to watch somebody play a game that's already been won or lost and that nobody honestly cares much about seeing again, unless you happened to be the one scoring an impressive goal.

"Okay," Sam answered.

"We can watch while we play." He shuffled through some DVDs and fed one into the player, then returned to his checkers.

Concentrating on the next few moves, Sam didn't look up at the screen for a while. When she did, she couldn't figure out what she was looking at. "Who's that little bitty kid?" she asked.

Ty had also been staring at the board and not at the TV. He gave a jolt of recognition. "Oh, that's an old video of me playing with my dad. I stuck in the wrong disc." He reached for the eject button.

"Wait a minute," Sam said, suddenly interested. She pointed to a figure in the corner of the screen. "Is that your dad?"

"Yeah."

"He looks like Ben, only bigger."

"Yeah." They forgot all about checkers, eyes glued to the screen. There was Ty as a tiny little squirt, Ben as a primary school kid, and Mr. Doherty. Sam didn't think she had ever seen a video of him before. Ty found himself lost in his memories. There were times like this when his dad felt so close he expected to see him walk through the door.

Ty had a thought. "Let me show you something," he said. Opening a drawer in his desk, he took out a box the size of a large cigar box, painted blue and decorated with stars and stickers and a drawing of a soccer ball. "This is a very special treasure box," he explained.

Sam's eyes grew wide. "Treasure? What's in it?"

"Important stuff. Not money, necessarily, but stuff I want to keep in a special place."

Sam was impressed. She didn't know anybody else with their very own treasure box. Ty opened the top and Sam put her face against his so she could see inside. There were papers and marbles and a few other things. The biggest item in it was a black book. Ty carefully took it out and held it up.

"This was my dad's Bible," he said.

"Wow." Sam whistled softly—another very non-girl thing she could do—and took it gingerly in her hands.

"Mom told me that Dad read from this Bible every morning before he went to work. And look, you can see he wrote all these notes and underlined places. Mom keeps it in her room but she lets me borrow it sometimes." Ty's memory—or the shadow of a memory—had transported him to the past. He could almost hear that voice, smell the scent of his dad fresh from the shower.

"You miss him?" Sam asked quietly.

"Sometimes."

"I know I'd be sad if my daddy didn't come home."

"That's why this is special," Ty said, putting his finger on the Bible. "It belonged to him."

The two sat without speaking, the chatter from the soccer DVD filling the quiet.

"Hey, wanna see something else really cool?" Tyler exclaimed. "Come on!" Sam put the Bible on the desk and followed Ty downstairs, through the kitchen, and toward the sewing room his mother used as her office, workroom, and hideaway.

"Where are we going?" she hollered.

"You'll see."

"Ty, don't go far, honey, supper's almost ready," Granna reminded him.

"I'm going to show Sam the letters," he yelled without slowing down. He waved and hurried on. Sam hustled after him, sensing adventure ahead.

Ty breezed into the room and opened a storage closet. "This is where my mom keeps her important stuff," he explained.

"Are you sure it's okay for us to be in here?" Sam asked, a little nervous.

"Mom said me and Ben can look at these anytime we want as long as we're careful."

"At what?"

"Just hang on and I'll show you!"

It was a surprisingly big closet stacked with boxes in different sizes and colors, mostly labeled with markers: Christmas, baby clothes, everything Ty wasn't looking for. There was one stack of things that had been his dad's, but he couldn't tell it from the rest by looking. He worked his way through the closet, methodically reading labels as he went.

"What are you looking for?" Sam asked excitedly. "Let me help." She turned a big box in the middle of a stack slightly so she could read the label, causing the whole stack to start teetering.

"Look out!" Ty warned. The kids jumped aside as the stack tumbled down into a pile. Luckily it didn't knock over the next stack, which could have started a very messy chain reaction. And also luckily, the boxes were all shut tightly so none of them spilled. The children each picked up a box and started restacking.

"Wait!" Ty exclaimed. He looked at the label on the box Sam held: *Letters to God*. "This is what I was looking for. Sam, you're a genius."

"I know," she said playfully.

Ty dragged the box out to the middle of the room, took a deep breath, then unfolded the flaps.

"What is this stuff?" Sam asked.

"These are my dad's letters to God," Ty explained.

"Letters to God? No way!" Sam squealed in an uncharacteristically girlish voice.

"Way!" Ty declared, triumphant. "Wait 'til you see."

Using both hands, Ty carefully lifted a dog-eared notebook out of the box. On the cover was a handwritten label that said *Letters to God*. He rubbed his hand gently across the surface, then held it out for Sam to see.

"*Letters to God*," Sam read aloud. "That's wild." She peeked into the box. "There's a whole stack of them." She reached in and pulled out a handful. They were different colors, sizes, and shapes: some nice-looking diaries, some spiral notebooks, some writing tablets.

Ty opened the one he was holding and turned slowly through the pages. The sight of his father's handwriting and the feel of the diary in his hands always gave him goose bumps.

"Did your dad really write all these letters to God?" Sam asked in astonishment. "Did he ever get an answer?"

Ty said nothing. He'd just come to a page he remembered as though he'd seen it this morning. There was the stick figure he'd drawn of himself and his dad and the sunrise the last morning of his father's life.

"I remember this one," Ty said at last. "Mom has read it to me lots of times."

Dear God,

I especially thank you for days like this. What a joy it is to have a special little guy like my Tiger. Thank you for allowing me to see this before starting my day. It reminds me of all I should be thankful for!

"Ty! Sam! Time to eat! Come wash up!" Granna called.

"We'll finish later," Ty said.

"Promise?" Sam couldn't bear to leave these mysterious letters unexplored.

"As soon as we eat," Ty assured her.

As fantastic as Granna's pork tenderloin was, Ty and Sam had a hard time concentrating on the meal and, as far as Granna and Ben were concerned, seemed to be in a rush, though they insisted they weren't. Once the meal was over, they carried some of the diaries to Ty's room and out to the hideaway he'd built to work on special projects and for when he wanted to be by himself.

He called it "the fort." Outside his window was a flat section of rooftop with a decorative railing around it. A big live oak branch hung over the spot. It wasn't meant to be a porch, and there wasn't any door to it, but it was a perfect place to have a snack, hang out with friends, or do anything he needed to do in private. Sam and a few other select friends could visit him there without even going through the house. There was a ladder to the roof and they could climb right up. Ty usually crawled out the window, which was what he and Sam did this time.

They sat side by side on a couple of well-worn lawn chairs, reading Patrick's old notebooks. "Did God ever answer any of the letters?" Sam had waited impatiently since before supper for an answer about that.

Ty strained to remember. "He told me something about how God sort of answered them, but not exactly. He didn't get letters back."

"Do you think he actually mailed them?"

"I don't know. Not that I ever saw."

"Seems like he wrote about everything."

"Yeah. Listen to this one:"

Dear God:

I get so tired working two jobs. I miss eating dinner with Maddy and the boys, and I hate being late for their games. Ben loves football, and Ty is a natural at soccer. I want to cheer them on, but I've got to be at the bank mopping floors! Help me remember you love them even more than I do. You're there for them when I can't be. You know my heart, and you know their needs. I trust you to make it all work out.

"Here's one," Sam said.

Dear God:

Christmas is coming again. I know the boys are still small, and I want them to enjoy the presents and excitement of the season. But help me show them what Christmas really means. Make Maddy and me good examples of the love you show us every day, so we can show it to them.

They took turns reading until Sam's granddad called for her to come home. She climbed down the ladder. "See you tomorrow," she called out as she waved good-bye.

"See ya, Sam," Ty answered, then went back to his reading. When it got too dark and cold outside, he carried the notebooks in and read some more until his head started to hurt. He was so focused on the letters that he didn't feel the pain until it was too late. If he ran to the bathroom, Granna would worry and call Mom at work. So he hopped through the window to the fort and threw up outside on the grass, where it wouldn't show.

Hi and Merry Christmas

The fall soccer season was long past, the last leaves had fallen, and Ben spent a brisk afternoon hanging Christmas lights on the Doherty front porch. He'd been at it for hours, and now the dark was about to catch up with him. There was still a lot to learn before he could do it as well as his dad used to, but Ty hadn't helped matters any. When Ben had helped his father, it had seemed like the two of them did it so much faster. Ben had retrieved the lights, untangled the cords, then handed them up so his dad could hang them on little nails along the roof. Now Ben was on the ladder where Dad used to be, and Ty sat on the porch fumbling with a wad of wires and lights and getting them even more scrambled.

"Come on, Ty, geeze," called Ben from the ladder. "Do I need to call Sam to come help me?"

Ty ignored him and kept working but couldn't seem to make any headway. Ben climbed down the ladder with a huff and yanked the lights out of his hands.

"Now that's no way to treat your brother, especially at Christmas." Their mother had appeared out of nowhere, standing in the front doorway.

Ben jumped. "Sorry," he said without meaning it.

"Don't tell me, tell him." Ty hadn't moved since Ben took his lights, his hands hanging loosely in his lap.

Ben leaned over and gave him a brotherly punch in the arm. "Sorry, punk." Ty smiled. "We'll finish tomorrow."

"Supper's on the table," Maddy said.

Suddenly animated, Ty darted past his mother. "I'll beat you in the house!" he said, ending with a war whoop.

"Cheater!" Ben yelled, running to catch him.

When Maddy followed them in, she found Ty sitting on the stairs holding his head.

"Another one?" she asked. Ty could only nod as he crossed his forearms over the top of his head.

"I'll get you something," she said and headed for the kitchen. Granna sat at the table, food already dished onto her plate, clasping her hands. "I'm not waiting much longer," she called out jovially as Maddy went by. "I think mold is starting to grow on the bread."

Maddy opened the cupboard above the stove and rummaged through the various medicines, cold remedies, and vitamins.

"Another one?" Granna asked.

"Afraid so," she said, digging around for the right bottle. Spotting it, she checked the label carefully and poured a dose into a small plastic cup, darting from the kitchen as quickly as she had entered.

Maddy handed the cup to Ty, then walked him up to his room. He flopped onto the bed and she helped him into his pajamas. He hurt too much to care what he slept in.

"Is it about the same?" she asked gently.

"Worse," he whispered.

Maddy finished dressing him for bed. "Do you want your

dinner now or later?" He held up a silent hand, signaling for quiet. "I'll be back to check on you," she whispered.

Granna and Ben were already eating. "I don't think it's an allergic reaction like his doctor said," Maddy told them. "That allergy prescription hasn't helped a bit. And there's no rhyme or reason to when he gets sick."

"Honey, you've got to stop thinking the worst," Granna said. "If you're really that worried, though, maybe you ought to take him back to the doctor."

"It might just be a waste of time and money," she admitted, "but I think I'll do that after the holidays." She looked over at Ben, who continued chowing down. At least he seemed healthy, his fork steadily working its way from plate to mouth and back again. Ben had not only put up the outside lights, he'd hung lights on the Christmas tree too, again with a little help from Ty. Patrick had always considered that a man's job, and Ben took his responsibility for it seriously. Maddy let the boys do it any way they wanted to; she wouldn't dream of "improving" on their work—until after they went to bed, that was, and then she'd go around the house straightening and centering the decorations.

It seemed like no time before the big night was upon them. Christmas Eve always gave Ty butterflies—the good kind—in his tummy, and this year was no different. He waited eleven long months for December and then forever and a day for the night of the twenty-fourth. His dad had told him the whole story about baby Jesus the last Christmas they had spent together, but that didn't stop him from looking forward to the arrival of Old Saint Nick. Part of the Doherty holiday tradition had become recalling Christmases past, when Dad had been with them.

They'd scarcely gotten up from the supper table when Ty had his pajamas on. The sooner he did, the sooner they could observe another of his favorite Christmas traditions. Though the big family celebration was on Christmas Day, everybody got to open one present on Christmas Eve: a present Ty picked out for them. By the time Granna and Maddy came out of the kitchen, Ty was on the floor, half-lying under the tree, looking for the right gift for each person to open. Christmas music played merrily in the background.

"Hurry up, you guys," Tyler yelled from under the tree.

"Hold your horses, young man," Granna advised. "Those presents aren't going anywhere." She sat down in the recliner, tilting it all the way back after a day of holiday cooking and package wrapping. Maddy and Ben followed close behind and sank down on the sofa.

"So," Maddy asked, "what have you picked out for us this year?"

Ty handed each of them a present, saving the largest for himself.

Ben was quick to notice Ty's present was bigger than the other three combined. "What's up with that, pipsqueak?" he teased, pointing at the big box.

"I couldn't find a smaller one," he explained happily.

Ben looked at his mother as if to say, "Can you believe that!"

"The rule is you get one present tonight," Maddy reminded them, "and that's one present. There's never been a limitation on size." Ty gave his brother a smirk.

"Then I want to pick my own," Ben said.

"That's only fair," Granna agreed. Ben put the present Ty had handed him back under the tree and took another, much larger.

"You open first, Mom!" Ty begged.

Maddy tore off the wrapping on her gift to reveal a white box. She opened the lid and pulled out a cream-colored hand-knitted sweater, lifting it high for all to see. "I love it!" she said. Ty beamed with satisfaction. "How on earth did you get this?"

Tyler cut his eyes slyly over to his grandmother, who turned away. "It's a secret," Ty said in a conspiratorial whisper.

Ben opened next. To Ty, it seemed like it was taking him forever to rip through the paper. "Geeze, Ben, you'd think you'd never opened a present before."

"You open 'em your way, I'll open 'em my way," Ben answered, savoring the moment. Under the wrapping paper was a plain brown box. Ben opened it and started digging through wads of tissue paper, then paused, surprised, eying whatever was at the bottom. "No wonder it was so heavy," he said.

"So?" Tyler questioned.

Ben held up a rock, obviously hand-painted by a seven-year-old, with a smiley face and hair made out of a cotton ball. "Is this some kind of a joke?" Ben asked. Ty looked confused. Maddy glared at Ben.

Granna saw the disappointment in Ty's face. "Well, I think it's beautiful!" she declared. "I hope I get one. I'd love a 'Mr. Rock.'"

"You got it, Granna," Ty said, relieved. "It's a rock star for my brother the rock star!"

"Oh, I get it," Ben said, playing a few enthusiastic licks of air guitar. "We'll have to jam together!"

The last Christmas ritual of the night was the one everybody looked forward to most. Maddy went into the sewing room—off-limits to everybody else for the time being, because that was where she and Granna wrapped presents—and returned with a worn-looking notebook. She settled on the couch with it and waved the boys over. Ben snuggled on one side and Ty on the other, while Granna wriggled in between Ty and the arm at the end and threw an afghan over all of them.

"Everybody ready?" Maddy asked. The three heads huddled around her all nodded. The notebook fell open at a place near the middle.

"Are you sure you don't want to hear a different one this year?" she asked the group.

"No! No way!" the chorus responded. "We want this one," Ty declared. "Might as well stick with it," Ben added.

"All right," Maddy said. "This was your daddy's last Christmas letter to God." She ran her fingertips lightly over the page he had once held in his own strong hands. He'd probably written these words at their desk in the bedroom while she was catching her last five minutes of rest. What she wouldn't give to have those five minutes back right now.

Maddy held the book at the best angle to catch the light and read aloud.

Dear God,

Another Christmas is here. The older I get the closer together they seem! In a little while it'll be pandemonium, but before the Christmas crazies start, I want to thank you for the best present any man could have—my family. Christmas joy comes in all sizes, and you've given me everything I ever dreamed of under one roof. A beautiful, faithful, adoring wife.

A single tear ran down Maddy's cheek.

A talented, artistic, healthy first-born son.

Ben leaned his head on his mother's shoulder.

And my Tiger, who wants to know if Santa brought any presents to baby Jesus.

Ty smiled a wry smile. That line embarrassed him a little. After all, he was only three then.

> *Actually that's a pretty good question. I hope you'll answer it for him sometime. It's going to be a great Christmas for us all. May you grant us many more wonderful Christmases together. And Merry Christmas to you too.*
>
> *Faithfully,*
>
> *Patrick*

Snuggled under his blanket, hands tucked under his head, Ty listened to the sounds of the night and wondered what tomorrow would be like. Christmas Day! He wondered if Santa got his letter and whether he'd bring him everything he had asked for. He wanted another autographed soccer jersey and that new pro-model soccer ball his mom had been promising but never delivered on. Maybe even a bicycle. He hoped Santa would come through.

There was a knock at the door. Without waiting for an answer, Ben stepped into the room and climbed up beside his brother. The boys sat on the bed in silence for a moment, each lost in his own thoughts.

"Do you think about him a lot?" Ben asked at last.

"Yeah," Ty answered. "But I don't remember much. Most of what I know I picked up from the videos and letters and everybody talking about him."

On Christmas Eve the boys slept together, mostly so neither would get a head start opening presents in the morning. Whoever woke up first was supposed to wake the other, then they went in together and woke up Mom. If they went downstairs without her, she'd have a fit.

"Wanna pray before we hit the sack?" Ty asked.

"I don't think so, but thanks anyway." Ben got in bed and crawled under the covers beside his little brother.

"But if you don't talk to God, how can he know what you want, what you need?" Ty insisted. "How can he forgive you for bad stuff you've done?"

"I don't know, but it's Christmas Eve, and I don't want to think about it now. Besides, if God's out there, why doesn't he give us our dad back for Christmas? He ought to know that's what we want."

"But the Bible says the Lord is our shepherd, that he gives us everything we—"

"I don't want to talk about it any more." Ben pulled the covers up over his head and rolled over.

With a shrug, Ty clasped his hands together and went ahead on his own. "Dear God, I'm so glad it's Christmas. Thank you for all the presents I'll get in the morning. Thank you for loving me when I'm good and even when I'm not. Bless Mom and Granna and Ben. And tell my dad hi and Merry Christmas and that I love him. Amen."

Christmas morning came awfully early for Maddy and Granna, who had been up until 3:15 trying to figure out how to put Ty's bike together. Maddy forced an eye open and looked at the clock: 7:00 a.m. *That's odd*, she thought to herself. Ty was always up at the crack of dawn on Christmas. She grabbed her robe, slid on her scuffs, and padded down the hall.

Maddy tiptoed toward Ty's room and eased open the door. Ben, still sound asleep, was hogging the bed, one arm across his brother's chest. Ty lay beside him wide awake, perfectly still, his hands holding his head.

"Tyler, it's Christmas!" she said softly so as not to wake Ben. "Ready to rise and shine?" With a low moan, Ty lifted Ben's arm off his chest and looked at her pathetically.

"Another headache?" she asked. He crawled out from under the covers and sat on the edge of the bed. "Oh, sweetie, I'll get you some medicine." *Oh no, not on Christmas. Not on his favorite day of the year.* She brought him an allergy pill and a pain reliever, then went down to help Granna fix Christmas breakfast.

The meal was another family tradition—homemade cinnamon rolls, fresh fruit, and hot cider. It was festive, filling, inexpensive, and the boys loved it because it was mostly sugar. Granna was taking the first batch of rolls out of the oven. The Christmas tablecloth, printed with trees and packages, was unfolded on the table, and she had already stacked the Christmas plates on the kitchen counter.

"You timed it perfectly," she teased as Maddy came in. "The hard work's done. All you have to do is cut up the rest of that fruit and set the table." Maddy picked up a knife and a cantaloupe. "Are the boys still asleep?"

"Ty has another headache. I gave him some medicine, and he's going to rest some more."

"Poor baby," Granna clucked. "And poor you. I wish you wouldn't worry so much."

"That's what Carol and Jamie Lynn say." She put her hands on her hips and leaned in toward her mother. "'Honey, you know just enough about medicine to be dangerous!' is what Carol tells me. They think we should keep an eye on him, but not assume the worst."

"Now why on earth would they ever expect you do to that?" Granna asked with a gentle poke in the ribs.

"One! Two! Threeeeeee! Merry Christmas!" The two boys came flying down the stairs. Ty seemed fine, which was better than she could say for herself, thanks to that blasted bicycle.

Pulling himself around the bottom of the banister, Ty dashed to his new bike. "Awesome! Awesome!" was all he could say in his excitement and delight. It was sort of like Ben's, which he admired, but different enough to be distinctive.

Maddy and Granna exchanged winks. "At least Ben's video game didn't come in pieces," Granna whispered, as Ben picked up his big gift with a shout of delight.

"Sweet!" he said as he tore open the box and got ready for video action. "The latest and greatest!"

The rest of the day was a picture-book Christmas. No snow, of course — it had only snowed once in Orlando in fifty years. But Ty had no more headaches, the kids spent all day with their new presents, the fragrance of cinnamon and cloves lingered in the air, and nobody looked at a clock all day.

A few days later, Ty rode his new bike over to play with his friend Colt Turner. Besides being soccer teammates, they enjoyed a little one-on-one basketball in the driveway. It was a close game. Ty brought the ball in from the backcourt, dribbled around Colt, and fired off a perfect layup.

"Ten to ten!" Ty yelled excitedly.

"No way," Colt insisted. "I have twelve."

Ty stopped under the basket, sweating and winded. He bent over holding his head.

"What's the matter? Tired of getting beat?"

"You're not winning; it's tied."

"Nuh uh," Colt insisted.

Tyler shook his head slowly. "Maybe you ought to pay more attention in math class," he said. Then, with no warning, he dropped the ball, grabbed his stomach, and retched on the pavement directly under the net.

"Way to go, puke breath," Colt taunted. "Now we can't play anymore!"

"Sorry," Ty said weakly. "I think I better go home."

"Okay. See you tomorrow."

That night as Tyler lay in bed, his mother sat beside him rubbing his back.

"Did you get too hot?" she asked.

"No," he answered, "it was the same headache I always get. My stomach starting feeling a little weird and then I tossed my cookies."

"I bet you just got too hot. Do you feel okay now?"

"Yeah, I feel fine."

When I Am Afraid . . .

Maddy glanced away momentarily from the wild, enormous crowd celebrating on TV.

"What did you say, sweetie?" Ty had asked a question, but she'd been concentrating on the commotion in Times Square.

"I said I'm tired," Ty repeated in a small, weary voice. "I want to go to bed."

In the light of the television screen, Maddy could see a tousle of blond hair poking up out of the nest Tyler had made in a quilt snuggled on Granna's lap.

"It's only nine o'clock," she said. "Don't you want to see the ball drop?"

"Not really."

"What a nooge!" Ben grumbled from the other end of the couch. "What's with you, Ty? We've waited a whole year for this and now you're gonna miss it?" He plunged a hand into the quilt to give him a poke. Tyler let out a yip.

"That's enough, Ben," Maddy ordered. It had been a pretty good day overall. No reason for the boys to start going at each other at this hour.

Ty climbed down out of Granna's lap, trailing a corner of the quilt behind him, and stood in front of his mother.

"You sure you don't want to stay up with us?" she asked again. Ty shook his head. "Okay. I'll be up in a minute to tuck you in."

When the next commercial came on, Maddy climbed the stairs to Ty's room. It seemed like only yesterday that he was so little he looked lost in a full-size twin bed. The new year made her think about it. He was starting to get lanky and lean. Her baby was gone and a handsome, high-spirited boy had taken his place. Tyler was going to have his father's build to go along with her coloring and features.

She pulled the covers up under his chin like he liked them. "I can't believe you're not going to ring in the new year with us," she said. "But I guess you just need the rest." She leaned down and kissed him on the forehead.

"Mom?"

"Yes, sweetie?"

"Does God celebrate New Year's?"

She thought it over. "I don't think God runs on the same calendar we do. It's like there's no time, or that time is never ending. Some people think there's no past or future in heaven, that from God's point of view everything is the present. Does that make sense?"

Ty crinkled his nose and furrowed his brow. He was actually more confused now than before. "I'll have to think about it. But thanks anyway."

"You're welcome, Tybo. Sweet dreams. See you tomorrow." Maddy turned once more to go but felt a tug on her robe.

"Can you tickle my back?"

With a smile, she lay down beside her son and started running her fingers up and down his spine. In less than a minute, he was out, his face peaceful in the dim light from the hallway, his breathing deep and regular.

Maddy went back downstairs and joined Ben and Granna for the final stretch of Times Square partying. At midnight the big crystal ball descended as hundreds of thousands of merrymakers counted down the last seconds of the old year. The moment arrived, the band played "Auld Lang Syne," and Maddy, Granna, and Ben stood to drink a toast with sparkling apple cider.

"Happy New Year, Mother," she said, giving Granna a hug. "Happy New Year, Benjamin." They exchanged greetings all around, took their seats again, and had another sip or two of cider. Suddenly everybody felt very tired.

"You go on to bed, honey," Granna said. "I'll clean up. It won't take two minutes."

"Thanks, Mom," Maddy answered. "I'll take you up on that. We'll consider it a late Christmas present."

Maddy headed upstairs to her bedroom, the stairs creaking in their familiar, comforting way. She and Patrick had bought the house before Tyler was born, a roomy, solid, inviting place with its wide, welcoming front porch and a garden arbor with a swing out back, close enough to town to be handy but far enough away to be quiet.

All it really needed these days was a husband and father.

Tired as she was, Maddy couldn't settle down. She always thought so much about Patrick during the holidays. In some ways their time together had been so short — only three New Years for the four of them as a family — but in other ways it was like he had always been a part of her.

Lying in bed waiting for sleep to come, she thought about the first time she ever saw him. She was a skinny freshman at Crockett High, and he was one year ahead. She'd gone to the last baseball game of the season with some girlfriends; they hadn't been to a single one all year and figured they might as well check it out.

Even playing against their crosstown rivals from West End, baseball was pretty boring, but she hung in there pitch after pitch after pitch. Finally, it was the bottom of the last inning with one out and runners on first and second. Crockett was losing four to two.

Up to the plate stepped a player Maddy hadn't noticed before. Not only was he incredibly good-looking, he moved with such grace and confidence. Taking his warm-up swings in the batter's box, he idly scanned the bleachers. She saw him look at her and detected a definite reaction: a little hesitation, a hint of a smile on that stern game face. She smiled back and gave a little wink. He did a double-take, then shook off the distraction and tried to get his head back in the game, but not before the pitcher burned one over the middle of the plate.

"Stee-*rike*!" called the umpire.

The batter set his jaw; his eyes narrowed. He was not going to let one like that get by him again. If only he had one more chance....

The pitch was right in the sweet spot again. With a metallic *ping* he sent it flying up, up over the center field fence and into the trees. The crowd jumped to its feet, clapping and yelling, with Maddy yelling louder than anyone. As he rounded third, he looked up into the stands again—looking for *her*—and their eyes met again. She felt butterflies in her stomach. She still got them every time she thought about that day.

Before the school year was over, Maddy and Patrick were an item at school and their friendship had grown into love. That summer Patrick made two vows to her: to marry her and to get a baseball scholarship. By baseball season of his senior year he had a whole drawer full of scholarship offers but was still waiting on word from the school he dreamed of most—the University of Texas. *Hook 'em horns!*

That meant he and Maddy would be apart while she finished her senior year at Crockett. They'd talked about it and both believed it would work out. If they really loved each other, their relationship would survive.

Then came the day everything changed: the day she found out she was pregnant. She and Patrick had only gone all the way once and promised each other they'd never do it again until their wedding night. They would be faithful to one another, faithful to their beliefs, and faithful to God's commands. Only once, but in a few weeks the signs were there and the results were positive. When she got the call from the doctor confirming the home test, she ran out of her house and onto the porch in a panic, afraid, ashamed, disoriented, collapsing in sobs on the steps, her head buried between her knees.

Looking up, she saw Patrick rounding the corner. *Not him! Not now!* What could she tell him? It was all too sudden. He slowed down as he came closer.

"I guess you've already heard."

What? This made no sense. Maddy couldn't focus. "What? Heard what?"

"The scholarship! A full ride at the University of Texas! I just got the letter—"

"I'm pregnant."

He rocked back on his heels like he'd been slugged. After a long moment, he sat down beside her on the same step, but leaving a space between them.

"I'm not taking the scholarship, Maddy," he said.

Maddy stared at him. "Don't you want to think about it—"

"I don't have to think about it. There's nothing to think about." His voice sounded surprisingly assured and reassuring. "I'm staying here with you and our baby. We're going to be okay."

Looking into his eyes, she saw the same sparkle she'd seen that day on the baseball field. Felt the same butterflies. And she knew he was right. They were going to be okay. In fact, the way it turned out they were much more than okay, blessed beyond anything she could have imagined. It wasn't the life she'd planned on, but it was wonderful just the same. Maddy loved being a wife and mother, loved making their home a comfortable, welcoming refuge for Patrick, Ben, and later for Ty as well. For ten years her dream house was the setting for a dream marriage.

Then everything changed again the night Patrick was killed.

Her memories drifted into dreams as Maddy settled down to sleep at last in the first dark, starlit hours of the new year. Everybody called this the holiday season, and though Maddy hadn't been on duty at the hospital for days, she'd worked even harder than usual to make Christmas as festive for her mother and the boys as she could. It wasn't until she'd climbed under the covers that she realized how tired she truly was.

And yet even the deepest sleep can't keep a mother from hearing her child in distress. Aroused to a pinpoint of consciousness, Maddy couldn't tell at first if she was dreaming or if that was the sound of Ty heaving in his bedroom. She opened one eye to peer at the clock. *Three a.m. Must be dreaming.*

Then she heard it again. Maddy threw on the hall light and went into Tyler's room. The stench met her at the doorway. She flipped on the light and saw him lying in a puddle of vomit.

"Oh, Ty! Ty!" She sat him up, pried him out of bed, and walked him toward the bathroom. Granna intercepted them in the hallway and followed them in.

"Everything okay?" she asked sleepily.

"If you call throwing up all over the bed 'okay,' then I guess so," Maddy answered, preoccupied.

As Maddy got Ty out of his pajamas and sponged him off with a warm washcloth, Granna changed the sheets and hustled the dirty ones into the washing machine.

In a few minutes Maddy tucked him back into bed, feeling his head. "You don't feel warm," she told him. "You had another headache, didn't you, sweetie?"

Ty rolled over. "Yes." He looked drawn and pasty even in the dim light. "My head hurts."

"I told Granna I was taking you back to the doctor after the holidays, and this settles it. Something's not right. There's a bucket beside the bed if you have another emergency." Ty didn't move, didn't speak. She turned the light out and padded back to bed.

Heavy as her eyes were from exhaustion, she fought to control a rising sense of fear. *This isn't normal no matter how old you are. I don't care what that crazy doctor says.* She was having her struggles with God some days, but now she felt a deep need for his guidance. "God," she said softly, "you know how this scares me. Help me. Take away my fear. You're bigger and stronger than any fear can ever be. Please let this be just allergies or something else I can get a handle on. He's so young and he loves you so much. I know you love him, Lord. Touch him with your healing hand and make these headaches go away."

Praying made her feel better, but it didn't take away that feeling that something was very, very wrong. Sometimes she thought Carol was right, that as a nurse she knew too much. If she didn't have the medical knowledge about all that could go wrong, she wouldn't stew about it like she did. Still, of all the possibilities, one scared her the most: Ty's symptoms were consistent with a brain tumor. It was a way-out-there thought, but she couldn't shake it. There wasn't any history of cancer in her family or Patrick's, as far as she knew. Furthermore, she admitted to herself that, as any frightened mom might do, she was jumping to the most serious and least likely conclusion right off the bat.

A dozen diagnoses were more likely than that one. But what if it was a tumor? What if Ty had brain cancer? "Please, Father," she prayed on the edge of sleep, "let this be nothing." But there it was again: the sound of Tyler retching. She looked at the clock. Forty-five minutes. She pushed out of bed and got to Ty's doorway to find him leaning over the side of the bed, half making it into the bucket, half not.

"Well, that's better than in your bed again," she said, heading straight for the bathroom and a wet washcloth. She sat next to him, one hand on his back and the other holding the cloth on his forehead.

"Can I get you anything to drink?" Tyler shook his head. "Want me to lay with you?" Tyler looked up at her with those sad eyes he got only when he felt really bad. Maddy turned the light off and lay beside her sick little boy.

Less than an hour and he was heaving again, only this time nothing came out. Maddy tried to get him to sip a glass of soda, but he only wanted to sleep. Their miserable ritual went on about once an hour until daybreak. Maddy called the pediatrician's office as soon as it opened.

"What did he say?" Granna asked, standing at the top of the stairs in her bathrobe.

"He's more worried about dehydration than about the headaches or vomiting," Maddy reported. "He wants us to go to the emergency room."

"Now?"

"Yeah."

"Let me grab some clothes."

"You don't have to go, Mom."

"Nonsense. It's what grandmothers do."

"You're not leaving me here by myself," yelled Ben, who'd overheard.

Granna drove and Maddy sat in back with Ty, who vomited once more before they arrived at the ER entrance. Ben lifted his younger brother out of the van and carried him through the automatic doors to a row of chairs, where they sat while their mother filled out the paperwork.

They waited for hours, watching people stream in and out, some coughing, some bleeding, some crying, some unconscious. As time went by, Tyler became more and more alert and responsive, to the point where he acted like nothing was wrong.

"Great," Maddy exclaimed to her mother and Ben. "All that ruckus I caused and they're going to think I'm one of those crazy, overreacting mothers!"

"Doherty!" a nurse called out in the flat voice nurses seem to save for times like that.

"The doctor will be with you in a moment," she added robotically, leading the four of them to a small, bare examining room and closing the door behind her. After another long wait, a handsome man in a white lab coat entered. He didn't look a day over twenty-five. Maddy wondered how he could possibly be old enough to have graduated from medical school. *He'll just call it a flu bug or allergies and send him home with a handful of prescriptions.*

"I'm Doctor Pittman," he said breezily, offering his hand. "What seems to be the problem today?"

Maddy opened her mouth but her thoughts were too jumbled up, crowding around to get out all at once, so that she couldn't seem to say anything at all. Should she talk about the headaches first? The vomiting? Her feeling that the allergy diagnosis was wrong? The sense she had somehow that things were getting worse? In the end she didn't say any of those things. From way down deep, another thought blasted past all the rest and, before she knew what was happening, she heard herself say, "Check him for a brain tumor."

The doctor tried not to show how stunned he was. "And what makes you think he has a brain tumor?"

The torrent of thoughts came tumbling out and Maddy launched into her explanation, sentences spilling and falling over each other. She talked about the months of headaches, how at first they happened only occasionally, but had gotten more frequent and intense. Now he was waking up at night vomiting. "I want him checked for a brain tumor," she repeated. The doctor gave her a frozen half-smile. "Are you going to do it," Maddy continued, "or do I have to go over your head?" Granna's eyes widened. Ben put his hand over his face.

Dr. Pittman kept writing until his notes caught up with the end of the narrative. Then he stood squarely in front of Tyler and looked him up and down with an experienced eye. "You look pretty tough to me, pardner," he said. Ty grinned. "Let's take a listen." He blew on his stethoscope to warm it, then listened to the boy's heart and lungs. "Innards sound okay." Ty grinned again. He went on to check his reflexes, then his eyes. "Stand up here and do your flamingo thing for me." Ty cocked his head. "One foot." The doctor demonstrated. Even Maddy chuckled. With an understanding nod, Ty balanced first on one foot, then the other.

"Your son seems to be fine now," Dr. Pittman concluded.

"Is this how you figure out if he has a brain tumor?" Maddy asked, unconvinced.

"Mrs. Doherty," the doctor answered, trying to hurry things along without being obvious about it, "if Tyler had a brain tumor, his balance would be affected. His equilibrium, the movement in the eyes, pupil dilation—something would indicate abnormality. He doesn't show any of these signs. I'm happy to say he seems perfectly healthy."

"But he plays soccer," she said, as if that explained something. The doctor looked at her with an "and so . . . ?" expression. "He's very athletic." Her intensity was tinged with desperation. "Whatever you ask him to do, he'll do. If he's a bit off balance, he'll compensate. If he can't walk a straight line, he'll make adjustments. He's beating your test, Doctor."

Dr. Pittman looked puzzled, his eyes shifting from Ty to his mother and back. Picking up his clipboard, he began to write again. "All right." He knew when he was licked. "I'll order a CT scan. We'll schedule it for tomorrow." Maddy let out a long sigh of relief.

That night Maddy slumped on the edge of Granna's bed, staring blankly out the window. "I know that look," Granna said. "There's something big on your mind."

Maddy tried to sort through the thoughts that still crowded her head. "I'm worried," she said simply at last.

"'When I am afraid, I will trust in you.' Psalm fifty-six, verse three," Granna quoted.

Maddy sat up to face her mother. "Mom, have you ever just had a feeling about something and knew you were right even though you couldn't prove it?"

"I knew you were pregnant with Ben before you told me."

Maddy hung her head. Granna put her finger under her chin, raising it enough to look into her eyes. "I didn't say that to make you feel ashamed. I said it because you asked. I'm just saying I felt the Lord speak to me and knew without a doubt I had a precious grandson inside your body." The corner of Maddy's mouth showed a hint of a smile.

"Mom, I know it sounds crazy, but I've known for a while something is wrong with Tyler, something more than just headaches. I really think it's a ..."

Granna placed her fingers against Maddy's mouth. "Shhh. Don't say it." She reached for her Bible, flipped it open to a marked page, and began to read aloud. "'In God, whose words I praise, in God I have put my trust; I shall not be afraid ... This I know, that God is for me ...'"

The words swept across Maddy like a cool breeze. She lay back on the bed listening, hanging on every word. When her mother stopped reading, Maddy wanted more. She felt like a teenager again, like her mother's wisdom and warm embrace would fix everything. Like God hadn't forgotten about them after all.

"Let's just wait and see, shall we?" Maddy nodded her head. "Let's pray." Maddy nodded again. After the prayer she stood up, tears brimming her eyes. "Thank you." They embraced.

"It's going to be all right," Granna assured her. "Stop thinking the worst, okay?"

"Okay." Maddy got up to check on the boys. They were both sleeping like rocks.

Chasing a Shadow

The next twenty-four hours seemed like twenty-four years. It was all Maddy could do to push back again and again against the fear that welled up inside her. She told herself she was not going to panic. But their appointment wasn't until 7:30 that night, and every minute dragged by at an agonizing pace. Maddy walked the floor, watching the clock and waiting impatiently for the time when they could leave for the hospital. *What if I am crazy? Better crazy than Ty being misdiagnosed.*

They got to the hospital at 7:15. Ben slumped in a chair in one corner with his iPod while Ty played a video game, looking and acting perfectly normal. Maddy and Granna browsed aimlessly through old magazines or stared at the walls. At the sound of her name, Maddy popped out of her chair like an overwound spring. She and Ty trooped back to an examining room. As she walked through the doorway, Maddy looked back at her mother, who pointed heavenward with a reassuring smile.

Ty lay on a narrow bed in front of what looked like a giant metal donut. The bed would slide into the donut hole far enough to get his head in. The machine would then produce 3-D X-rays that could help the doctors see if there was a tumor or some other abnormality in his brain. The technician explained the procedure to him and his mother while hooking Ty up to an IV.

"You're going to feel a stick, little man." Tyler winced. His mother winced with him.

"For this to work, you have to lie completely still," the tech went on. "We can give you some medicine to relax you, if you want."

"That's okay. I won't need it," Ty answered bravely, craning his neck to look at the big machine.

The procedure took fifteen minutes. The whole time, Maddy badgered the technician with nervous questions, but the only thing she really wanted to know was when they would have the results.

"Tomorrow afternoon sometime," the tech told her. "Because it is so late, the film won't be developed until morning." Another long and sleepless night.

Maddy had been thinking hard about what her mother said earlier about God, and about Psalm 56. Her mother was right. God was there for her and Ty. He had to be. If he wasn't there, nobody was. Late that night she knelt beside her bed, tears streaming down her cheeks. She believed in her heart what the Bible said about not being afraid, knew that God loved her and loved Ty, but she was still petrified—desperate and afraid for her precious son. She prayed that the test would prove there was nothing wrong. Prayed that the dark feeling of doom gripping her heart was completely groundless. Prayed that if Ty really was sick, God would heal him right now. When she finished and tried to stand, her legs were completely numb: she'd been kneeling for an hour. Rolling into bed, she slipped between the sheets and was soon asleep.

The next morning Ty woke up with another headache. He had them almost every day now, and they seemed to be getting worse. But between bouts of whatever this was, he seemed incredibly resilient and looked and acted perfectly normal. In less than an hour he was out in the yard kicking a soccer ball back and forth with some of the neighborhood boys.

Maddy was watching the boys out the window as the phone rang. Taking a deep breath and saying a quick prayer, she picked up the receiver.

"We found a spot, Mrs. Doherty. A shadow," the voice on the line said. Her heart felt like lead. "We're going to need him back tomorrow for an MRI."

Slinging the receiver in the direction of the base, she missed it entirely and fell to her knees, sobbing. All that prayer. All that Bible reading about trusting the Lord and being protected. And now this. What did it mean? She felt the roller coaster headed into a dive. *Why, Lord? In the name of Jesus, why?*

"Why are we here again, Mom?"

Maddy tried to answer Ty's question, but the lump in her throat wouldn't let her. Instead she walked in silence with him through the doors to the radiology department. This visit was a bit different from the last one. Today's machine looked a lot like the one before, but instead of X-rays it used powerful magnets to produce an image of a person's insides. It showed greater contrast in soft tissue than X-rays could, so doctors could take a clearer look at spots that appeared fuzzy in X-rays, especially on organs. They would also do a spinal tap to see if there were cancer cells in his spinal fluid.

The technician wanted to sedate Tyler this time. "Most kids can't lie still long enough for this one," he explained to them both. "And if he moves, we have to start all over." One look in his eyes convinced Maddy that Ty didn't want to be sedated.

"Think you can handle it, Ty?" He nodded.

"He's fine," she said to the technician. "If he can't be still, then you can give him something."

The tech went to work, manipulating the huge machine so that it scanned every inch of the boy's head, lines of light moving slowly across his face. In this moment of crisis, Maddy prayed silently, asking God that the CT scan be nothing but a mistake. That's what she wanted desperately to believe, but she was having a hard time believing it.

Outside afterward, the two of them walked toward the van. "Race you!" Ty yelled and darted off, glad to be out of that thing and full of pent-up energy. Caught off guard but not to be outdone, Maddy sprinted as best as she could, yet lost by a country mile as mothers always do.

She opened the door and flew into her seat. "I'll beat you buckling!" Grabbing the belt, she yanked it across her lap, sliding it smoothly into the latch. Everything was a contest today.

"No fair!" he shouted, fumbling with his belt.

"Spoil sport! You can't win all the time!"

"But you cheated!"

"You mean like you did?"

"Did not!"

"You were halfway to the van!"

He tried to look indignant but couldn't hold the giggles in. The contest ended in peals of laughter as they headed for the ice cream parlor.

There would be another long night waiting for test results.

Maddy settled in for the vigil in front of the TV, glancing over at the phone every few minutes. With each tick of the clock her chest got tighter. She already felt like an elephant was standing on her. It took all her concentration to breathe.

Granna stood up. "We're going to a movie," she announced.

"Do you think we should?" Maddy asked with concern. "What if they call?"

"You gave them your cell number, didn't you? If there's no answer at home, they'll try the cell. You can put it on vibrate."

The four of them saw some movie, but when it was over, Maddy couldn't have told anybody what it was about or even the title. All she could think about was an MRI test result on a piece of paper somewhere that held sway over her entire world. What was on it? When would she know? Did she write the phone numbers down right on the hospital forms?

The ride home was quiet, Ty dozing in the backseat, Ben plugged into some noisy Christian rock.

Maddy's cell phone rang. She gripped the wheel, knuckles white. Her blood turned to ice. She looked at her mother, who closed her eyes, her lips moving in silent prayer.

The phone felt incredibly heavy in her hand. She couldn't press the talk button, and she couldn't not press it. Her thumb moved across to the round black button in the center.

"Hello?"

As she listened, her breathing became heavier and more rapid. Her hands started to shake. "Oh please, God!" she murmured, scarcely above a whisper, as the tears came.

"Pull over," her mother insisted, watching her face intently.

Maddy pulled over to the shoulder and put the car in park. Jostled, Ben plucked one earbud out and asked, "What's up?" No answer. "Granna?"

"Not now, Ben," Granna said with unaccustomed sternness. "You'll wake Ty up." He looked at her, looked at his mother, shrugged his shoulders, and plugged back in, his gaze fixed out the window.

Maddy sat alone, looking around yet another waiting room. *Old. Every person in here is old. Surely they all can't have what Tyler has. But what does he have?* She revisited the signs she had seen over the past five months, things nobody else ever seemed worried about. Now here she was, waiting to see a neurosurgeon for what surely couldn't be very good news.

Maddy followed a nurse down the hallway to a cluttered office with papers stacked high on the desk and piled on the floor. "The doctor will be right in," the nurse said cheerily. Maddy looked around at the diplomas, certificates, plaques, and framed articles on the walls. Dr. Chester Gaylin. Whoever Dr. Gaylin was, at least he evidently knew what he was doing, even if he was a bit of a slob.

The doctor came in and introduced himself. Youngish, efficient, all business. Maddy noticed he never looked her in the eye. Was that bad manners or bad news?

"Mrs. Doherty," the doctor began, "we've looked carefully at your son's CT scan and MRI. He has medulloblastoma."

Maddy mouthed the word silently. *Medulloblastoma.* A kind of brain tumor. She hadn't wanted to be right.

"This is a tumor in the cerebellum, the lower back part of the brain," Dr. Gaylin went on, "the part that coordinates muscle movement." Maddy knew all that but she listened carefully anyway. She wanted every scrap of information she could collect, and she wanted it now. "Most cases are in children under ten. They may wake up vomiting. They have headaches in the morning or during exercise, then the pain goes away and everything's fine." *I knew! I knew but nobody would listen.*

"The cancer has already spread to his spinal fluid, in addition to being in the tumor and the lining of the brain," Dr. Gaylin recited. "We'll give him steroids to decrease the pressure on his brain. That should do a lot to help the morning headaches. There are only around three hundred and fifty children a year diagnosed with this type of tumor," the doctor continued. "And these tumors grow fast. But with aggressive treatment—surgery, chemotherapy, radiation—the prognosis for recovery is good."

"Three hundred and fifty a year," Maddy repeated. "So there's really no one experienced in treating them then, is there?"

Dr. Gaylin seemed to ignore her question. He launched into an explanation of the surgery Tyler needed to remove the tumor, then the radiation to kill any stray cancer cells at the site and chemotherapy as well. "We need to have the surgery done sooner rather than later," he concluded.

Maddy nodded her head as though she were listening and turned to look out the window. *No child should have to go through any of this.*

"So, three o'clock next Friday is all right?"

Maddy shook off her daze. "What?" She didn't care for his all-business attitude.

"Next Friday, three o'clock, for surgery?"

"I think so. Yes."

"My office will call to confirm."

She stood in a hurry and left the room as fast as she could. She raced through the hallway and flung open the outside doors, gasping for air. Maddy sat down in the van but was in no condition to drive. She was crying and couldn't seem to focus on anything. Her son had brain cancer. What would happen now? And why, Lord, did it have to be him? Why couldn't it be her?

"God, he's only seven!" she begged, staring blankly through the windshield. "Take me instead! I've had a life. I've had children. I've had happiness and fulfillment. I'm not nearly as afraid to die as I am to think that Tyler ..." She broke completely down, her head on the steering wheel, her hands limp in her lap, crying as only the brokenhearted can cry.

Maddy had no idea how long she sat there before the sound of an ambulance siren stirred her. She lifted her head and started the van. But where would she go? She wasn't ready to go home yet but didn't feel like going out anywhere. Driving aimlessly at first out of the parking lot, she found herself heading across town to a place she'd visited many times, though not much recently while things had been so crazy.

She turned slowly in through the gateway, idling past the headstones. She usually came here by herself because she didn't want the boys to think this was where their father was. They knew he was in heaven, waiting for them to join him. Maddy parked and walked slowly toward Patrick's grave under a big oak tree. She sat down in the grass and leaned her head against the gray granite headstone.

"Patrick, what's happening?" she asked softly. "What did I do that was so wrong that God would take you from me, and then put me through the agony of watching our precious son suffer? What am I supposed to think? What am I supposed to do? I've felt so abandoned, but I know, Patrick, that God is out there and he's not against me. Not against us. He's for us. But it's so easy to forget that when your husband is dead and your son may be dying."

Maddy got irritated sometimes when her mother kept

encouraging her to pray, but a prayer felt like the right thing to do at the moment. And so she prayed.

"Lord, be with Ty through all the trials that lie ahead. I don't understand your will. I can't; I'm only human. But please be merciful to him and to all of us. Take his pain away. Relieve his suffering. And help us love you and praise you no matter what. Give us the strength to submit to your will. Bless us. Let us feel your presence. Be with us every step of the way."

A warm breeze stirred around her, waving the grass and lightly rustling the branches of the mossy oak overhead. It felt almost like arms wrapping around her, warming her on this cool winter day. She turned her face into the breeze and smiled, then looked up at the brilliant clouds against a dark blue sky.

"Thank you," she said.

Lowering her gaze, she focused again on Patrick's headstone. "You'd better put in a good word for him. After all, you're his daddy."

You Are Listening

As Ty crawled into bed that night, he took one of his dad's journals out of the treasure box and brought it with him. He had just started flipping through the pages when a tap on the window interrupted him. It was Sam. She'd come up the ladder and through the fort as usual. He closed the journal, hopped out of bed, and raised the window. Sam clambered into the room, dressed in a terrycloth robe, knit hat, and sneakers.

"Where have you been lately?" she asked, concerned. "There's only one week left of Christmas break, and we've still got lots to do."

"I know, I'm sorry. I've been at the hospital."

"Was somebody sick?"

"Not really sick. Mom wants to find out why I get headaches. And besides, I've been puking a lot lately."

"Hey," she said cheerily, "I've puked before. You get better. Nothing's wrong with you; you're fine. Come out as early as you can tomorrow, okay?"

"Okay."

Sam climbed out onto the roof and nimbly picked her way to the ladder. Shivering from a blast of January air, Ty shut the window and crawled back into bed with his journal, snuggling deep into the covers.

He'd heard his mother read a lot of his dad's letters by now and was reading some of them himself. The ones he couldn't read yet he looked at anyway, picking out words he knew and getting the gist of them. He felt his father's presence so strongly as he went line after line, page after page, struggling sometimes with the handwriting, wondering what his dad must have felt as he wrote. He so clearly remembered the morning his dad told him it was hard for him to pray the usual way and so he wrote letters as his way of praying. Tyler thought praying was easy. Writing seemed a lot harder because it took so long.

Why couldn't he do both? Maybe his dad was on to something. It couldn't hurt to try it. He could ask God to help his mom. She worked so hard for him and Ben, and sometimes she seemed so tired and lonesome. Maybe God could cheer her up. Since Ty had been on vacation, he had no idea where his school notebook was. He turned to a blank page in the back of his dad's journal and started to write.

Dear God,

I don't know if this will work or not but my dad did it, only he never really put his letters in the mailbox to you.

I want to ask you something. My mom seems really unhappy, like she's scared about something. Can you talk to her and help her to not be scared? She thinks I'm sick, but other than getting a headache sometimes, I feel okay. Thanks.

Love,

Tyler

PS—Please tell my daddy hi for me, or maybe you can let him read this letter.

Now what? Did you put a letter to God in the mailbox like an ordinary piece of mail? He'd have to think about that one.

Downstairs, meanwhile, Maddy paced up and down the living room as Granna watched. *Her son had brain cancer.*

"You have to trust God," Granna said with quiet intensity. "You know that. I know you do. Your faith is being tested. Ask him to help you through this."

"But it's so hard."

Granna stood and took her hands, then led her to the couch and guided her down. "God knows how you feel, sweetie. He's stronger than cancer, stronger than your fear, stronger than anything. Lean on him, Maddy. Confide in him. Let him be your rock."

Maddy looked lost and bewildered. "Four years ago my husband was killed by an irresponsible idiot. Today my seven-year-old boy is diagnosed with brain cancer. I don't see how God can come up with an answer for that."

"That's just it. We don't see. We can't see what God sees because we're not God. That's where faith and trust come in. We have to have faith, and then trust him to do what's best even if it looks all wrong from our point of view."

"I'm sure you're right, Mother. I just need to think about it."

If she couldn't yet deal with the spiritual questions that troubled her, Maddy could at least tackle the practical ones. Those she understood, and dealing with them gave her a sense of accomplishment. First thing next morning, she called the HR department at the hospital to get started on her request for a leave of absence. She'd be away a month at least for surgery and chemo, maybe longer, and needed to make sure all the paperwork was under way.

She also had to face the question of her creditors. She already struggled to keep up with her bills every month. Being away from home to take care of Ty meant she wouldn't be working and wouldn't be available to field their calls or answer their letters about why they weren't being paid. She decided to take the initiative, go on the offensive, and call the people now before they called her. Lining up the bills in order of importance—the biggest, oldest ones at the head of the line—she called every company. Overall, they were surprisingly courteous, thanking her for explaining the situation and telling her to pay what she could as soon as she could. The one sticky situation was with her car loan. She was already two payments behind. The person on the line said she sympathized with Maddy and they would be as flexible as their standards allowed. But if she got more than three payments behind, they would repossess the van. That was simply company policy.

Finished with that chore, Maddy sat at the table with her head in her hands, a cold cup of coffee beside her. Over and over she replayed her discussions with Dr. Gaylin. Yes, he was an expert, but everything seemed to be happening in such a hurry. Even if she wanted to look at other alternatives, what could she do about it now? Who else could she talk to? Where else could she go?

Maddy went in to work that night so another nurse could fly out of town to visit her sick father. She sat with Carol and Jamie Lynn in a rare moment of calm. They'd had a busy shift, but all the babies and their mothers were quiet for the time being. Carol glanced up from a stack of patient charts.

"How's it going, honey?" she asked Maddy. "You haven't made a peep all night."

"Just thinking," Maddy answered, staring at a sheet of updated doctors' orders but not reading them. "I don't know what to do about Ty's surgery. Everybody seems so gung ho about this doctor and everything, but I feel"—she paused, looking for the word—"weird about it. I know I should be glad to have a diagnosis and for things to be moving along. I'm just—scared."

"I hear that," Jamie Lynn replied. "I'd feel the same way if it was my boy. And, Maddy, you've done your homework on this. Checked out the doctor, the hospital, the procedure. Everything is solid."

"I know. I just keep thinking there are only a few hundred cases of this a year. How can anybody get to be an expert when it's so rare?"

"Honey, I'll tell you what you should do. You've talked to us, right? You've researched everybody's accreditation from here to next week, right? You've been on the computer looking for answers, right?" Maddy nodded. "Have you been praying, girl?" Maddy nodded again.

"What you need to do is keep praying and keep looking. Don't give up. Listen to your heart—that's God talking to you, honey. Pray for God to guide you and keep looking and asking questions until you know you have the answer. Google and ye shall find!"

"I'll do it," Maddy declared, newly inspired.

As soon as she walked in the door after work, she sat down at the computer and typed *medulloblastoma* into the search bar. Her initial search pulled up all the now-familiar websites, but there were one or two she hadn't noticed before, which led to others that were filled with the latest updates about this rare and dangerous kind of tumor. She soaked everything up eagerly. After what seemed like only a few minutes, she felt a hand on her shoulder.

"Sweetie, what are you still doing up?" Granna had come down to put on the morning coffee. "You need to be in bed."

"Mom, look at this." Maddy's eyes were glued to the screen. "New lists of the hospitals that handle these cases. Lists of surgeons that do these operations and how many they do in a year. All kinds of new research about rehab and recovery and remission rates. It's a gold mine!"

She read eagerly. On the one hand, it was empowering to know so much. On the other, it was depressing: most of the individual stories had sad endings. This was a very bad type of cancer to have.

Maddy kept working, nodding off from time to time, then catching herself and forging ahead, driven to find more information, determined to feel that she'd done everything she could for her son. Who had treated the most cases? Who had the best track record? Wherever they were and whatever they cost, Maddy would find them.

Finally, exhausted, Maddy shuffled into the kitchen to drink what was left of her mother's coffee. She picked up the pot then set it down again, leaned against the counter, and started to cry. These were such big life-or-death decisions. And she was so alone. *If only Patrick were here. He'd know what to do.* She sat down at the table, sleepy, scared, lost. But Patrick wasn't there. What would Patrick have done? The same thing her mom and Carol kept telling her to do: pray. He would be on his knees right now. She eased herself down into a kneeling position on the floor, braced her forearms on the edge of the tabletop, and had a long conversation with God. By the time she was finished, the coffee was ice cold. She poured it out, started a new pot, then resumed her quest.

For the rest of the weekend Maddy probed the farthest reaches of the Internet, stopping only for catnaps and a sandwich or two. Late Sunday afternoon she found herself looking at a screen full of information about a brand-new program at St. John's Children's Research Hospital. Compared to some of the hospitals she'd been reading about in Los Angeles, Vancouver, and London, St. John's was practically next door—a couple of hours down the interstate in Port Charlotte on the Gulf Coast. She and Patrick used to get mailings from them and would send in a small contribution every year.

The more she read, the more excited she got. St. John's specialized in very sick children, including cancer patients, now including medulloblastoma, and all treatment was free. Maddy jumped like she'd been shocked and let out a little yelp of joy. Every patient they served was treated for free in exchange for participating in clinical studies.

Granna wandered in just then. "You've got quite a marathon going," she observed. "What's the latest?"

"Look at this!" Maddy exclaimed.

Granna read the screen over her shoulder. "Unbelievable. It's a miracle." Maddy remembered her prayer at the table. *You were listening. You are listening. Oh, thank you, God.* Maddy tapped out an email to St. John's explaining Ty's condition and asking if they could help.

Monday morning, Maddy felt like a different woman. Bounding out of bed, she grabbed a robe and went downstairs to make pancakes for breakfast. Ben drifted in a few minutes later, his shaggy hair a rat's nest. "What's the occasion?" he asked, sniffing the air.

"I just felt like making breakfast, that's all," Maddy answered brightly.

As Ben poured himself a glass of orange juice, Ty came in following his nose. "What smells so good?" he asked.

Granna was hard on his heels. "What I want to know is, how much did you sleep last night?"

None of them could remember the last time they were all up so early to enjoy a homemade breakfast, all in a cheerful mood, and generally thinking the world looked pretty good. Ben had just shoveled the last bite of pancakes, drenched with syrup, into his mouth when the phone rang. Tyler raced to answer it.

"Hello?" he chirped. "Sure. It's for you, Mom, some doctor's office."

Maddy took a deep breath and grabbed the receiver. She was surprised to hear an unfamiliar female voice with a heavy Indian accent.

"Doctor who? Rashaad? Spell that, please." She listened for a moment. "Yes, I sent that email." As the others around the table watched, Maddy's face passed through a whole catalogue of emotions, from annoyed to curious to incredulous to unbelievably happy.

"Tomorrow!" Maddy suddenly blanched. "Like, the day after today? Shouldn't I talk to the other hospital first? His surgery's already scheduled." She listened some more. "All right, yes, thank you, I will. Bye."

Her eyes looked like dinner plates. "What?" Granna demanded, all but jumping up and down. "What, what? Who was that? What's up?"

"That was Dr. Rashaad at St. John's Hospital. She got the email I sent about Ty. She wants to see him tomorrow!" Maddy was trembling with excitement. "I don't know what to do!"

"I do!" Granna declared. "This is what you asked God for, isn't it? Well, here it is!"

"But it's so sudden! And what about everything we've already got set up with Dr. Gaylin?"

The phone rang again. Maddy jumped a foot. *They've changed their minds.* She snatched the receiver. "Hello? Yes, speaking." She listened intently for a moment as a smile crept across her face, then hung up.

"O ye of little faith," she said aloud but also to herself, bubbling with excitement. "That was Dr. Gaylin's office calling to put Ty's surgery off a week. I guess we're going to St. John's!"

"But I thought it was so important to have the surgery right away," Granna said, concerned.

"That's exactly what Dr. Rashaad said," Maddy answered pointedly.

Ty hadn't told any of his friends what was up yet. Now it looked like he would miss a big chunk of school. Tomorrow Christmas vacation was over, and if he wasn't in class, Sam would worry. After breakfast he went upstairs and called her.

"I'm going to the hospital for an operation," he said.

"An operation?" Sam exclaimed, duly impressed. "When?"

"Tomorrow."

"I'll be right over."

A minute later Ty heard a *tap, tap, tap* on the window. He raised the sash and Sam climbed inside. She got right down to business.

"An operation, huh?"

"Yeah. I have cancer." Sam started and her mouth fell open. She didn't know exactly what cancer was but knew it was bad. "The operation is to do something about my headaches and all the puking. Then I have special medicine to take afterward. Mom says we'll be gone between one and two months."

"That's an awful long time."

"Yep." Ty noticed the stars on one of his soccer posters and had a thought. "I wonder if my dad can see stars in heaven."

Sam shrugged. "I don't know."

"I wonder, do you see the backs of them from there, or the same side we do? Sometimes they don't look too far off, like if Dad could see them, he must not be too far off either."

"Are you scared?" She was the first person to ask him that.

"Nervous, mostly," he answered. "Remember when Ricky Anderson's grandmother got cancer and died? I wonder what it was like. I wonder if it hurt a lot." Sam shrugged again. "I hope you'll come see me," Ty said.

"You bet I will," Sam promised. "Hey, how about some checkers?"

Maddy packed all afternoon and into the night, making notes for Olivia and Ben while she and Ty were gone. Ben came through the hall, carrying his guitar case.

"You're home kind of late, don't you think?" Maddy prodded.

"Maybe. Been rehearsing for an audition." He watched her packing for a minute. "What's going to happen with Ty?" he asked suddenly. "Is he going to get well or not?"

His mother took his hand. "I don't know. What I do know is that we're going to trust God and get through this."

"Trust God?" Ben repeated sullenly. "Trust him to take care of Ty like he took care of Dad?" He grabbed his guitar and stalked out of the room.

"Ben!" As Maddy followed him upstairs, she heard his bedroom door slam. The door was covered with posters and signs

Ben had collected over time. In the middle was a big reflective sign in yellow and red reading "Danger! Biohazard!" Maddy knocked. "Ben!"

"What."

She opened the door. Ben was sprawled on his unmade bed with the guitar case beside him. "Look, I know you're mad," she said. He crossed his arms and looked out the window. "I'm mad too. But it won't help us to be mad at each other." Ben turned his head to look at her. "I don't know why your father was killed, Ben. I'll probably never know. But if we knew everything, we wouldn't need faith. One thing I do know without a doubt is that I love you more than you can possibly imagine—you'll see when you have a child of your own one day—and God loves you even more than that."

Ben held out both his arms to her like he had when he was a baby, and she rushed to hug him.

After a short, fitful night interrupted by bursts of nervous energy, Maddy was up early again to load the car and get on the road. "Ready for the big adventure, Tybo?" she asked as the two of them had quick bowls of cereal.

"You bet," Ty answered.

"No headache this morning?"

"No, I'm good to go." Maddy took it as a sign things were going to improve.

She went up to Ben's room to tell him good-bye. Of course, he was late getting up, as usual. She sat on the side of the bed and put a hand on his shoulder. "Time to rise and shine."

Ben rolled over to face her, and instead of the usual sour

expression he had a trace of a smile. "It's going to be okay," she said. "We're going to get through this. I came to say bye, and I hope you and Granna will come visit a lot." She kissed his cheek.

Ben sat up in the bed, wide awake. "Mom, let me come with you," he said. Taken off guard, Maddy wasn't sure what to say. Was this surly teenager trying to be selfless and helpful? "You know you could use me there—to help, I mean," he added.

"But, sweetie, we've got to leave right now," she explained.

Ben got up—he was fully dressed—and bounded toward his closet door. "Voilá." Opening the door, he took out a duffel bag, packed and ready to go.

"What about school?"

"Granna already called. They'll give me a week. I'll take my books and fax in my tests."

"You rascal!" She gave her son a mighty hug and headed downstairs with him close behind.

Granna stood beside the door, her suitcase at her feet. "You don't think I'm going to stay here by myself, do you? If you do, you've got another think coming!"

The family arrived in Port Charlotte with an hour to spare, so they checked into their hotel, then headed over to the doctor's office. The whole crew—Ty, Ben, Maddy, and Granna—went into a large examining room with two windows and plenty of chairs. Obviously, at St. John's they were used to making these examinations a family affair.

After only a minute, an olive-skinned woman with black hair and eyes the color of black coffee stepped in. "You must be Tyler," she said, looking at him. Maddy instantly recognized the voice of Dr. Rashaad. She held out her hand and Ty shook it. "I understand you've been having headaches, young man."

"And tossing my cookies too!" Ty added.

"I've been looking at your tests and reading your file." She turned to include the whole room. "I still think immediate surgery is the way to go. This is an aggressive tumor, but we can take aggressive action. There's a lot we can do. But I have to tell you, as with any brain surgery, there are risks. Ty could lose some or all of his memory."

Ty made a face. "So I have to learn my math tables over again?"

"Let's hope not," the doctor answered. "But you might possibly have to learn to walk and talk again. In some ways, it could be like starting over. When it comes to the brain, we can't predict what will happen—we can only tell you the possibilities. It will take seven to ten days to recover from the surgery, then chemotherapy and radiation will take another month or so. At least we can do the chemo at Memorial Medical, Maddy, close to home and where your friends can keep an eye on him. And you."

"Close to home is good," Maddy repeated. "But what are the chances of the cancer ... ?"

The doctor raised her hand. "We never use that word around here," she told her sternly. "The C-word? It doesn't exist. It's a negative word, and we only promote positive attitudes and positive healing. We'll see you for check-in tomorrow morning at six."

On their way out to the car, Maddy watched the boys horsing around the parking lot. *This is the last time I'll see them play together for a long time.*

"Let's go eat out someplace nice," Granna suggested. "My treat."

"Hey, Tybo," Maddy called out, "what would you like for dinner? Anything you want."

"Pizza!" Ty said, jumping up and down.

"Looks like you got off cheap, Granna."

Back at the hotel after dinner, the boys were still rambunctious. "Let's wrestle!" Ty hollered. "On the bed. Two minutes."

"Want your tail kicked one last time, eh?" Ben shot back, rising to the challenge. "You're on!"

Normally Maddy would never have stood for such behavior in a hotel room, but these were not normal times. Watching them, she remembered how they'd loved wrestling with their father. In seconds they had their shirts off and were going at it, giggling and grunting like two maniacs. . . . *And the last time I'll see this for a while.* She hated to make them stop, but after a few body slams and close calls with the furniture, she declared the match a draw and ordered them to get ready for bed.

It was going to be a long day tomorrow. The weeks ahead would be full of long days.

A Good Idea

Ty wasn't allowed to eat breakfast the morning of the surgery, and in a show of support, nobody else did either. Maddy and Granna were too nervous to eat anyway, making Ben the only one who had to exercise any willpower. At the hospital everything moved along with clockwork efficiency. Ty changed into one of those embarrassing hospital gowns that come open in back at the most inconvenient times, then the family waited only a few minutes before Dr. Rashaad came in, trailing two attendants behind her.

"Good morning, Ty," she said, nodding at the others. "All set?"

"Good to go," Ty answered. "But how long do I have to wear this thing?" He pulled at his sleeve.

"Not long, I promise," the doctor answered. "We can treat cancer of the brain, but we can't seem to do much about gaposis of the posterior." She put her hand on her backside and everybody laughed, breaking the tension.

"This will be a long surgery," Dr. Rashaad continued after the room went quiet again. "Seven to ten hours is normal. Every couple of hours I'll have one of the nurses call the waiting room and give you an update. She'll also call if anything important or unexpected happens."

An attendant came in, pushing a gurney. "Here's your ride, Ty," the doctor said. "Hop on." Ty was more excited than scared; his mother was more scared than excited.

"I love you, Tybo. See you soon," Maddy said in her most cheerful voice.

"Love you, Mom." She gave him a peck on the forehead. He reached up and hugged her neck. That was the instant she thought, in spite of everything, she would burst into tears in front of him. But she held fast.

"See ya, weasel," Ben said, holding up his fist.

"See ya, doofus," Ty answered, bumping fists with him.

As the bed started to move, Granna called out, "Wait a minute. One more thing. Everybody join hands." The family gathered round. Maddy felt hot tears on her cheeks. Ty wondered if his dad was watching. Ben had a fluttery feeling in his insides.

"Lord, protect Ty today, and help us all," Granna prayed, then looked at Ty. "You'll do fine, kiddo." The gurney started to move again. "We'll be right here when you wake up."

Ty rolled through a set of double doors and into another room. Whatever he'd been expecting, it was nothing like this. The place looked like Santa's workshop, filled with toys, with shelves along the walls stuffed with books and games.

A nurse was there waiting for him. She looked very nice, he thought. "See anything you like?" she asked with a wide smile.

"Do I!" Ty exclaimed, surveying the roomful of loot.

"Well, you get your choice," she said. "Anything you want."

"Anything?" he asked incredulously.

"That's right."

Ty thought long and hard. It was an important decision; opportunities like this didn't drop out of the sky every day. After narrowing the choices down between a checker set and a model car, he finally went with the game.

"Okay, I have to say that was officially the longest time ever taken to choose a toy," the nurse announced. "We'll give this to your mom to hold until you wake up."

A man who looked like a doctor came in and started talking to Ty. "I'm going to help you go to sleep before your surgery," he explained, fiddling with some tubes and other things. Ty jumped only a little as he felt a stick in his arm. "How far do you think you can get counting backward from a hundred before you fall asleep?"

"I can get to zero!" Ty declared confidently.

"Wow," the man said. "I'll tell you what, I'll make you a deal. If you get to eighty, you can have every toy in this room."

"You're kidding!"

"Honest," the man said, holding up his hand. "Just tell me when you're ready to start."

Ty took a deep breath. "Ready. One hundred, ninety-nine, ninety-eight ..." Before he got to ninety, he was out. The nice nurse picked up the checker set—and the car too. She'd make sure he got them both.

It was the longest day of Maddy's life. When the first call came at 10:00 a.m., she snatched the phone out of the cradle on the first ring. "Hello?"

"Mrs. Doherty, this is the OR nurse. Everything's going fine. The situation is just what the doctor expected, and I'll call again in about an hour."

Quick, efficient, no bad news. An encouraging report. As the morning went on, the three of them read, dozed, watched television, snacked—and looked at the clock about two million times. A little after 11:00, the phone rang again.

"Mrs. Doherty? Another update for you. Everything's still going fine, but it's taking longer than Dr. Rashaad expected. Nothing out of the ordinary to worry about. Someone will call again when we're finishing up."

In less than an hour, the phone rang again. *They're in trouble.* She grabbed the phone, gasping for air.

"Hello?"

"Maddy, Pastor Andy here, just calling to see how you are."

Maddy heaved a huge sigh of relief, chuckling at her own panicked reaction. "Okay, I guess. But you just scared me! I thought you were the OR nurse telling me something had gone wrong."

"No, only checking in to say we're all praying for you and wishing you the best."

The next call was from a neighbor on Laurel Lane. This time Maddy hadn't jumped up in fear. Talking with Andy had calmed her, and she realized every call she got that day wouldn't be from the hospital. Other friends called during the long wait with words of encouragement and made small talk to help pass the time. What would she do without such wonderful friends?

At 6:00, Granna abruptly threw her magazine on the floor and stood up. "I don't know about you, but I'm ready for something to eat. And I think in honor of Ty, it should be pizza. Who wants to go with me?"

"I do!" piped Ben.

"I don't feel like going out. You two go."

Granna and Ben cruised the neighborhood around the hospital and found a pizzeria. The food was far from excellent, but a huge improvement over the junk food they'd been nibbling on all day. The slices they brought back to Maddy remained untouched on the bedside table. A little after 7:30, the phone rang again. The hospital.

"Good news, Mrs. Doherty. The procedure is finished and everything went fine."

"They're finished! He's okay!" she shouted to the rest. "Thank you, God!" The operation had taken ten and a half hours. Now they'd have to wait and see what the aftereffects would be. They might be unnoticeable, or he might be disabled for life, or anything in between. All that seemed strangely unimportant at the moment. All that mattered was that he'd made it through and the doctor was pleased.

Within minutes they were at the hospital to meet Dr. Rashaad, who came into the waiting area exhausted but smiling, still wearing her green scrubs. "According to the scans, we got it all," she announced. "That's very good news. Now as far as the lining of his brain, there's nothing surgically we can do. We're hoping radiation and chemotherapy will take care of that."

"Where's Tyler now?" Maddy wanted to know.

"Still in surgery. They're stitching him up. We'll have him in recovery in a little while; then you can see him. I'll be back tomorrow to see how he's coming along." She shook hands all around and left them to their thoughts.

A few minutes later they were called to wait in an empty room. They heard the sound of wheels on the linoleum, the door opened, and in came Tyler on a gurney, completely motionless, tubes coming out of him and into machines that wheeled along beside him, his head wrapped thickly with white bandages.

Maddy could scarcely imagine what that little body had had to endure just now. "Stupid cancer," she muttered under her breath.

Ben and Granna went back to the hotel to get some rest while Maddy settled in to spend the night with Ty in his room. Between her own motherly apprehension and the frequent interruptions of the nurse, she never had more than a catnap. By morning Ty still had never moved. Ben and Granna returned after a fitful night themselves, and the vigil continued. It was nearly lunchtime when Ty finally stirred and made a low moaning noise. His head began to move slowly from side to side.

"Mom?" he said, scarcely audible. The three of them jumped up and hovered over the bed. One eye opened and then the other. A tiny smile appeared on his face. "Hi, Mom," he said faintly.

"Hey, sweetheart," she whispered back to him, patting his shoulder because it was the closest thing not wrapped up or plugged into something. He seemed to fade into unconsciousness and then come to again. "Know who this is?" she said, putting her hand on Ben's shoulder. Would he recognize his brother now? Ever?

Ty stared with a blank look, then gave the hint of a smile. "My dork brother."

"Hey, you're the dork," Ben answered. He felt like crying but didn't know why.

"Who's this?" Maddy asked, putting her hand on her mother.

"Granna!" he said, slurring a little.

"That's right, sweetie, Granna," Granna said. "And Granna's not going anywhere."

Throughout the day Ty became gradually more alert. As he talked more, she asked him about school and Sam and his other friends, and he knew them all. His memory seemed to be fine. He moved around more and even wanted to walk to the bathroom. A nurse helped him and wheeled his IV pole along. So far there didn't seem to be any of the dangerous side effects they'd been fearful of and watching for so carefully.

The next day Dr. Rashaad came in with a handful of booklets. "I know you like to have all the facts, Maddy," she said.

"Here's some good information on chemotherapy," she held up one of the booklets, "radiation, subcutaneous ports," waving two more booklets, "and some other things that will help." The doctor looked at Ty dozing peacefully. "We have a lot of good news here. But I've got to remind you that this is a very aggressive strain, and we've still got plenty of work to do."

Ty continued his impressive recovery. After three days he was walking two or three times a day, and his appetite continued to pick up. At the end of the week Dr. Rashaad came in to remove the big surgical dressing.

"Let's see what we've got here," she said, gently turning Ty to face the window and unfastening the bandage from behind. Maddy, Granna, and Ben crowded around to look.

"Excellent, excellent," the doctor said.

"Wow!" said Ben.

"I wanna see too! Let me see!" Ty said excitedly. The doctor took a small hand mirror out of a drawer and aligned it with the wall mirror behind them.

"There!" Dr. Rashaad declared.

Ty gaped at the sight. A bright red scar started at the base of his skull and went up in a straight line toward the top of his head, the stitch-staples making short dark lines across it at regular intervals. He'd scarcely had time to take it all in when he caught sight of his face in the mirror Dr. Rashaad was holding. He was fat!

"What happened to me? I'm fat!" he exclaimed, incredulous. "I look like Humpty Dumpty! That can't be me!"

"It's the steroids, Ty," the doctor explained. "They do wonderful things to help you get better, but this is one of the side effects.

"Am I gonna be like this forever?" Ty asked with alarm.

"No. Absolutely not," the doctor assured him.

"It's not so bad looking like the man in the moon!" Ben quipped.

"Ben, that's enough," his mother said with a scowl.

Granna and Ben went home that night. Ty and his mother would stay at St. John's for a few more days before starting chemotherapy and radiation at Memorial Medical. Collapsing into bed, Ben dreaded the thought of school after a week away—all the catching up he had to do, all the questions he'd have to answer about Ty.

Granna sorted a week's worth of dirty clothes and did laundry until she thought she must have washed every thread in the house. She put Ty's clean clothes away in his room, picking up a few things between the door and the closet. Retrieving a piece of paper from the floor, she saw it was a letter, but not just any letter.

Dear God,

she read in Ty's large, rounded, seven-year-old hand.

I don't know if this will work or not but my dad did it . . .

Under the letter was one of Patrick's dog-eared notebooks full of his letters to God. She read the page her grandson had written, then started scanning here and there through the notebook. One letter grabbed her attention, and then another. She sat cross-legged on the floor, mesmerized, devouring page after page. What a good man Patrick was. What a good father. What a loving, precious husband. In that moment she was prouder of him than she'd ever been.

"God," she said quietly, "I hope you know what you're doing." She caught herself. "I mean, I know you do. I guess what I'm saying is that if you're ever going to answer a letter from anybody, I hope it's a letter like this from a boy like this, who has known loss and pain at such a young age, and who loves you more and knows you better than a lot of older and supposedly smarter people."

She put the letter and journal back exactly where she'd found them and went to finish repacking.

Once he recovered from the surgery, Tyler was moved to Memorial Medical Center to spend the next four weeks. He bravely endured the treatments and exams, the discomfort of the process, the pain of his incision as the pain medication tapered off, and the loneliness of being away from all his friends: the soccer team, his class at school, the people at church, and the neighbors, especially Sam. People did come to visit but couldn't come often because of school and because Ty was tired or sick a lot of the time.

One morning after chemotherapy his mother said, "Well, Tybo, that's it."

Ty had been counting the days until he could go home but didn't realize the time had finally come. "That's it?" His face brightened. "You mean I'm done?"

"For now. You are done, finished, finito."

Ty let out a war whoop. It was the happiest and most animated his mother had seen him since before the surgery.

"Man, I can't wait to get home! To see Sam and Colt and John! And all the kids at school!"

"Well, today's the day!"

Suddenly Ty had a troubling thought. "But what about this?" He ran his hand over his head, completely bald as a side effect of the chemo. "I don't even have *eyebrows*! And I'm still fat. I look like somebody in the circus."

"It's going to be all right, Ty. You've gotten along fine with the other kids here. Nobody's made fun of you."

"Yeah, but they're fat and bald too, some of them. And they never knew me when I looked normal. Alex and other kids at school will make fun of me."

"Let's not worry about that today," Maddy said, touching her forehead to his. "Let's think about being home and getting better. Okay?"

"Okay."

When they pulled into the driveway, Granna and Ben were waiting for them on the front porch. They clapped as Ty got out of the car.

"You said you didn't want any hoopla," Granna called out, "but we decided the grand arrival was worth at least a little applause." There were hugs all around as the family swept into the house.

Getting ready for bed, Ty came across the letter he'd written to God right before he left for the hospital and the journal of his dad's that had inspired him. He'd written God mostly to ask him to help his mom. But his dad had written his letters about all kinds of things, including stuff he himself wanted or needed.

He crawled into bed with the letter and journal. The more he thought about it, the more sense a letter to God made.

"I could tell God how much I want to get better," he said aloud to himself. "And how I don't want the kids at school to make fun of me. And how I hope I don't puke anymore." If God knew everything, he knew why Ty got sick and whether he was going to get well. Maybe God would let him know somehow. And since his dad had written letters, that meant it was a good idea.

"But God," Ty continued, like he was having a conversation, "how do you get the letters? Do I just put them in the mailbox?" He pondered how mail could ever get to heaven. Mail he sent to Santa at the North Pole obviously got there. Not that God and Santa were in the same league, but if the post office could get a letter to St. Nicholas, why not to God?

"I'll try it," he decided. All it took was a stamp. And since Mom bought the stamps, he had nothing to lose.

Finding a Purpose

As he got ready to mail his letter the next day, Ty thought about how to address the envelope. If there were streets in heaven, did that mean God had an address? Granna said God was everywhere. If that was true, he didn't need an address. And so Ty simply wrote "To God." He put it in the box with the rest of the mail and watched from the window as Mr. Finley, the mailman, poked it in his bag with everything else. Easy as pie.

When the letter didn't come back after a few days, Ty mailed another one. He didn't know how long it took for God to get a letter, or even if he'd write back. This time he saw that Mr. Finley took special notice of his letter, but still put it in his pouch.

A few letters later, he hadn't thought of anything to write until late in the day. He was afraid Mr. Finley would come before he finished. Looking out the window from his desk, he saw Mr. Finley's mail truck at the end of the street and saw him walking up to the first house. Good! He was ready just in time. He licked the envelope and sealed it shut, hammering it with the side of his fist for good measure.

The glue on the flap tasted nasty. "Eeewww, yuck!" he exclaimed, wiping his tongue wildly with both hands. Then, just above a whisper, he told himself, "Don't barf! Don't barf!" It didn't take much these days to make him queasy. Bolting from his desk and down the stairs, he lost his grip on the envelope. As it floated through the stairwell, he paused on the landing to intercept it. Snatching it out of the air, he kissed it and sped on to the door. Opening it with a jerk, he jammed his letter into the mailbox, slammed the door, and ran back up to his room to watch through the curtain.

Walter continued along his familiar route. "Rooster!" Mr. Finley hollered from the sidewalk in front of the Baker house, then gave a quick whistle. "You out, boy?"

Linda Baker opened her door and grabbed her good-hearted but monstrous dog by the collar. "It's okay, Walter, I got him."

"Thanks, Mrs. Baker. 'Preciate it."

He stepped up to the porch, where Linda bent down — which was hard because she was very pregnant — to hold onto Rooster with one hand and reached up with the other to take the mail. "Thanks, Walter."

Next was the Perryfield house, where old Mr. Perryfield, Sam's granddad, sat waiting impatiently on the porch as always.

"Hey, Mr. Perryfield. Sorry I'm a little late ..."

"A *little* late?" he grumped. "I thought surely you'd been waylaid by bandits," he said, gesturing broadly. "I was about to give you up for lost. There's a storm coming, and my old hip is killing me."

"Sorry to hear that." Walter handed up the mail and went on his way.

He turned in at the next house, 244 Laurel, the Dohertys. He'd already fished their mail out of his bag and held it in his left hand. Bills mostly, and a magazine. He lifted the top of the mailbox with his other hand, felt inside, and pulled out one letter. Reading the address on it, he grinned and shook his head. Another one of those crazy letters. A movement caught his eye and he glanced up to see the curtain moving back and forth in an upstairs window.

Back at the post office, Walter threaded his way with familiar ease through the rear entrance and past bins of incoming mail waiting to be sorted, churning conveyer belts covered with packages, and workers scurrying in all directions. To the untrained eye it was chaos, but to Walter it was the familiar sight of a proven process humming along in perfect order. He was about to leave it all behind for two months of extended vacation, his reward for ten years on the job. And vacation started in eight minutes.

Before heading for his locker, he put his mailbag down and walked over to Lester Stevens's small, cluttered office. Lester wasn't there, but by the time Walter settled himself in a chair across from his big battered metal desk that took up half the room, Lester rounded the corner and greeted him with a smile.

"Walter, I thought you were outta here!" He looked at his watch. "Yeah, you've got seven minutes to go, but consider them a personal gift from me." Lester was a big bear of a man with a rich, deep voice. Older than Walter and a little more world-weary, he loved his job nevertheless, proud to have worked his way up through the ranks to postmaster of the branch.

"What a guy!" Walter shot back with good-natured familiarity. "I just want to check with you one last time about — "

"Walter," Lester interrupted, "I told you not to worry about it. We'll find somebody. You're a great mail carrier, but you're not irreplaceable for two months."

"I need somebody good, Lester," Walter said with conviction. "I've been on this route ten years. People depend on me. I've got a whole stack of Certificates of Excellence for attendance, punctuality—"

"I know, Walter, but it's slim pickings right now." He sat down and leaned his elbows on the desk.

"What about that new kid, Trevor?"

Lester shook his head. "He's slow as mud through a straw. He can barely handle his own route, and yours is longer."

"Maybe Kay?"

"Kay's got a month left on maternity leave." Walter opened his mouth, but Lester held up his hand. "And before you ask, Pete just got his knee scoped again."

For a man five minutes away from vacation, Walter Finley looked amazingly crestfallen.

Lester leaned in closer across the desk. "Walter, this is your time. You've earned every minute of it. Go! Enjoy! Stop worrying! I've got Carl calling District Seven." Carl Landers was Walter's crew chief. "You have my personal assurance we'll find the right fit. I promise."

Walter stood to leave, then hesitated. "Don't forget to tell them about ol' Rooster at 231 Laurel. Otherwise they'll be hightailing it for the nearest low-hanging branch. And old Mr. Perryfield at 234 Laurel will call and give you an earful if his mail isn't in the box by one. And—"

"Walter?"

"Huh?"

"Go. Now. Bye-bye." Lester held up his big palm and waved his fingers.

"Right, boss."

Walter made it to the doorway before turning around again. "One more thing."

Lester looked up at the ceiling. "Oh, Lord, give me strength," he mumbled under his breath.

Walter took a handful of letters from his pocket and held them out. "Two-forty-four Laurel. I can't stand to shred these, but they just keep coming."

Lester stretched across the desk and took the envelopes. On the front of the first one, in a child's handwriting, was one word in capital letters: "GOD." He shuffled through them.

Walter sighed. "It's like finding a kitten on your doorstep. You just can't walk away."

Lester stared a long moment at the little batch of envelopes. "How long has this kid been writing to God?"

"A while now. I get one every few days."

Lester nodded. "Leave them with me. I'll take care of them."

"Thanks, Lester. Thanks a lot."

"The best way for you to thank me is to get your hindquarters through that door and stop worrying."

His last burden lifted, Walter walked down the hallway with a bounce in his step.

As Walter headed off, Carl Landers came by Lester's doorway. Carl was short, wiry, intense, and tended to fret about things.

"Hey, Carl," Lester called out.

Carl stopped. "Hey, Lester. What's up?"

"We gotta decide what we're gonna do about Finley's route. He's out of here for two months. I know we're running lean. Did you hear back yet from District Seven?"

"Yeah, and they don't have anybody they can spare now. Said

they'd be able to help us in a couple of weeks when one of their guys gets back from vacation."

Lester hesitated, anticipating the reaction, then said, "What about Brady McDaniels?"

Carl's eyes widened. "McDaniels? I thought you were ready to can him, not give him the best walking route in the branch."

"Yeah, I know," Lester admitted, "I just ..." He fumbled for the right word.

"He's completely unreliable," Carl continued. "When we need him, we can't find him. He's missed four days this month."

"Four days isn't all that terrible."

"When it's only the twelfth?"

Lester knew the facts were not on his side. "Okay, you got a point." He gave a wry grin. "I don't know. There's just something there worth saving." He pondered the idea. "I think he needs a purpose, something he can work for, a goal. Maybe he slacks off because he doesn't have a purpose, and he can't find a purpose because he doesn't care about anything."

"How many chances are you going to give him, Lester?" Carl wondered, mildly irritated. This McDaniels guy wasn't always doing his job, and that meant the rest of his crew had to take up the slack.

"Frankly, I'm not sure," Lester replied. "I know it's a pain for your other guys when he doesn't pull his weight. But, well, let's just see, why don't we? If he completely falls apart, we'll juggle the route until Bishop or Matthews can get over from District Seven in a couple of weeks. How's that?"

"Okay, let's try it," Carl said, unconvinced. "You're the boss."

"Thanks, Carl. If it doesn't work, I promise we'll give him the boot and get somebody more solid in there right away. Deal?"

"Deal." Carl looked at his watch. "Gotta go check on the shift change." Warming just a little, he added, "And I hope McDaniels makes the grade."

"I hope so too." Lester watched his crew chief scurry down the hall and disappear around a corner.

Lester looked at the letters again. The envelopes were crinkled and smudged here and there like they'd been crammed in a pocket or drawer or grabbed in a hurry. Some had smiley faces, flowers, or other drawings. No two were exactly alike. Each had a first-class stamp carefully pasted in the corner.

Lester slit the first one open and started to read. It was written in pencil on lined composition paper very neatly torn out of a notebook. He stared a long minute at the paper in his hand. Maybe that black sheep McDaniels could find purpose somehow in a letter like this.

Dear God,

I watched a video of me and dad playing soccer. I don't remember him much but I think we had fun. Tell him hi for me and I love him. I hope he laughs in heaven. I wish mom would laugh. Maybe you could do something to make her laugh more. And make Ben (my brother) laugh too but not in that mean way he does some times. You are great.

Thank you. Love,

Tyler

PS: My medicine stinks, but I don't have to take my spelling test this week, and that's good.

As he refolded the letter, he absentmindedly wiped his brimming eyes with his thumb and forefinger and reached for the phone. Checking the number on his computer screen, he put his call through and waited. After four rings, a scratchy-sounding recorded voice said, "Hey, this is Brady. I'm not here. Leave a message and I'll get back to you ASAP or whenever."

Lester sat straight up in his chair and after the beep said, "McDaniels, Lester Stevens. We need you in here first thing in the morning to take over for Walter Finley. I will remind you that your shift starts at six a.m. sharp, and if you're smart you'll shoot for a quarter till. Do not be late. You've used up all your favors."

At that particular moment, Brady McDaniels of the US Postal Service was drunk, and rather enjoying it, as usual. He sat warming his favorite barstool—one from the end near the windows—at his favorite neighborhood establishment, Jack's. He had lost track of exactly how long he'd been there that evening or how many drinks he'd had, but he had no doubt there was time for one more and it would be the tastiest of the evening. Cigarette smoke wafted through the room and the jukebox pumped out one of last year's biggest hits.

"Ready or steady?" Jack asked a cluster of regulars watching TV at the other end of the bar.

"Ready!" Brady called out, waving his empty glass. Jack glanced his way as he served the other customers. His buddy Brady was sloshed. Again.

"Ready, ready, ready," Brady chanted, banging his glass on the bar. "Do I have to fill out a form or something?"

"Spoken like a true government worker," Jack said, walking the length of the bar and filling his glass. He set the bottle down on the counter and leaned in toward the unshaven face. "You need to go home and get a shower and a shave and a good night's sleep."

"Why?"

"Because you look like forty miles of bad road and you smell like a rabbit hutch."

"Thanks, Mom."

"Look at me, Brady." Brady looked. His steel-blue eyes were glazed and bloodshot. He still had the solid build of a Marine Corps sergeant, but his scraggly hair and sloppy clothes were a world away from military precision. "As your bartender, it's my job to tell you when you've had enough," Jack said. Then, more quietly, "As your friend, it's my responsibility."

Brady stared into his glass for a long moment. "You were there. You know what it was like."

"I know."

"Justin was just a baby when I shipped out." Jack nodded. It was a familiar story. "Sarah had to handle everything by herself. She was a real trooper, Jack." Jack nodded again. "I saw stuff in Iraq nobody should have to see. Kids my son's age blown to pieces. Couldn't even tell if they'd been boys or girls." He closed his eyes tight. "Every time I closed my eyes, there they were. This chased them off." He opened his eyes and held up the glass. "And you know, it tasted good too. After a while I guess I didn't need an excuse."

"Guys have different ways of dealing with the awful things that happen in the world," Jack said. "Some are better than others."

"To each his own."

"It's just that—"

Brady cut him off. "It's just that you seem to have trouble remembering you're the bartender, not my mother. And not my commanding officer. You are no longer Captain Jack Albritton, United States Marine Corps; you are Jack the barkeep. And I'm no longer Staff Sergeant Brady McDaniels; I'm a paying customer in this establishment."

"McDaniels, if you keep pushing people away—"

"Save it!" he said, loud enough over the music to turn some heads, then downed his drink in one gulp. Leaning over the bar, he came nose to nose with Jack and poked him in the chest with his finger. "Can it, Captain Albritton, sir." He pushed away from the bar, stumbling slightly, and navigated his way toward the door. A couple of steps before he got there, he stopped and turned around. "And by the way, the music sucks." Then he was gone.

Knowing he was impaired and couldn't afford to get stopped, he concentrated hard and drove slowly. He pulled into an empty space at the Windsor Arms Apartments and walked to the door, fumbling with his keys as he went.

On the outside, his apartment building was shabby but neat. Inside, it was shabby and looked like someone had detonated a bomb filled with dirty dishes and rumpled clothes. He tossed his jacket on top of the pile on the floor and scooped up a bottle of bourbon off the kitchen counter. Glancing around for a glass, all he saw were dirty ones. He uncapped the bottle and held it at arm's length.

"Whiskey!" he said triumphantly. "It's not just for breakfast anymore." He sat down in his recliner and took a pull from the bottle. As he drank, he noticed the blinking light on his answering machine. He took another swallow. One or two more, and it would be time for a nightcap.

Suppertime at the Doherty house was even more chaotic than usual. It was Maddy's first night back at work since Ty's surgery, and she had to leave for the hospital right when dinner was supposed to be on the table. It seemed like no matter how carefully she planned, Maddy ended up starting the meal too early or too late, or something else went haywire. She'd been trying to hurry up a casserole so she could at least serve it herself before she had to go. Flying down the stairs in her scrubs, she bounded into the kitchen to the sound of the smoke detector screeching as a sooty dark cloud billowed out of the oven.

Sliding on a pair of kitchen mitts, Maddy opened the oven door, pulled out a black, smoldering lump, and took it straight to the sink. "Rats," she said, frustrated with herself for botching dinner yet again. Scurrying in from the back yard, Granna grabbed a pair of dishtowels and batted the smoke away from the sensor.

"Another gourmet dish?" Granna asked loudly over the smoke detector's racket.

"Yeah, something like that." Maddy surveyed the carnage in the sink. She'd had such high hopes for it. Finally, the screeching stopped.

"Don't worry about it." Granna could see her disappointment. "You've got to get to work. Anybody can make a casserole, but not everybody can be a pediatric nurse."

"I just wanted to make the boys a nice dinner."

Her mother turned her around, pulled off the oven mitts, and put them on her own hands. "You have enough on your plate. Let me tonight. As full as my schedule is—tea with the queen and all—I will sacrifice the whole thing for you. That's what moms are for."

"Thanks a million. Promise you'll let me know if it gets to be too much."

Granna held Maddy's face between her mitted hands. "Don't you worry, precious—"

"Hot. Very hot."

Granna jerked the mitts away. "Sorry about that!" They both chuckled.

Maddy ran water over the charred dish in the sink and glanced up at the clock. "I gotta move!" she gasped.

"Go!" Granna said, giving her a hip bump and taking her place at the sink.

"Love you," Maddy said hurriedly, and headed upstairs to say good-bye to the boys.

"Right back at you," Granna declared. She watched her go, then turned her attention to the molten disaster in the sink. Maybe the boys would like fish sticks for dinner.

Maddy dashed up to Ben's room and knocked on his door with its "Toxic Waste—Keep Out!" sign collection. She could hear him playing his guitar.

"Busy. Come back later," he called through the door.

"Busy, huh? Are you finished with your homework?" She opened it a crack.

Ben didn't look up from the chord progression he was working on. "Not due 'til Friday."

"And what will you tell me on Thursday?"

"I'll think of something." He flipped his hair and looked up at her.

"No one likes a smart aleck, young man," she said sternly. "Get that homework done. And clean up this room," she added, gesturing around. "It's a disaster area. 'Toxic waste' is right. And give Granna a hand in the kitchen. She's trying to get some supper on for you guys."

"Sure thing, Mom," he answered in his too-familiar sarcastic mode. "It's not like I have anything more interesting to do."

She'd made a point of not acknowledging him when he used

that tone of voice. "In the sack by eleven, and check in on your brother, okay?"

Ben ignored her. She closed the door, walked quickly down the hall to Ty's room, and knocked. She heard a DVD player going.

As much of a hurry as she was in, she stopped a second to look at him. He seemed in such good spirits, and acted fine. If it weren't for that scar and his bald head, he'd be the old Ty.

"Hey, Tybo."

"Hiya, Mom." He flashed her a big grin. He was sitting on the bed, watching himself playing soccer. "Hang on just a second, I'm ... about ... to ... score!" He threw both hands in the air, then clicked off the TV to give his mom his full attention.

Maddy sat down beside him and rubbed his back. "Sometimes I think that gorgeous smile of yours is the only thing that keeps me going." He gave her an aw-shucks look. "Tired?"

"A little."

"Stomach okay?"

"Good to go."

"That's my boy. How about your— "

"Mom," Ty said with mock exasperation, "I'm fine. I'm good. I'm okay."

"Okay, okay. I've got to go to work now. But you know you can call me any time."

"Right."

"Granna will help you with your meds tonight."

"Okay."

Maddy leaned over and gave him an Eskimo kiss. "You know how much I love you?" Ty knew what was coming, but he loved it anyway. She held two fingers close together. "I love you this much."

"That's not very much," he said, going along.

"Oh, but it is," Maddy insisted, "because my love starts here"—she pointed at one index finger with the other one—"and goes all the way around the world and ends up right back here." She tapped him on the nose and then kissed it.

Ty grabbed her around the waist and hugged hard. "And this"—he squeezed with a grunt—"is how much I love you."

Maddy shut her eyes tight, then stood up. "Granna's going to make you and Ben something for dinner. I sort of messed it up."

"Wow. Really? You?"

"Oh, you hush!" she smiled.

"I'm not so hungry anyway."

"I know. But try to eat something."

"Okay. I just don't like getting sick when you're not home."

"I know." She didn't want the moment to pass, but she knew she must be unbelievably late by now. "I've gotta scoot. See you in the morning?"

"I'll be here," he said cheerfully. She kissed the top of his head and gave it a rub, then flew down the stairs to the van.

On the Cusp

Maddy walked quickly through the parking lot to the service entrance and stepped out of the elevator on her floor at 7:00 p.m. on the dot. Carol, still holding her dinner, had come up just ahead of her and stood talking to Jamie Lynn, who sat in a rocking chair feeding a baby.

"Well, lookee here," Carol exclaimed. "Welcome back, girl." She put down her dinner and pulled Maddy into a bear hug.

"It's so good to be back," Maddy said, her voice muffled by Carol's ample embrace.

"How's our tiger?"

"He's good." *As good as a little boy can be after brain surgery, thirty radiation treatments, and four weeks of high-dose chemo.* "But we're home for a month before the next round."

Carol and Jamie Lynn grimaced at the list. Maddy took off her coat and sat down in front of one of the computer terminals. Carol pulled up a chair beside her. "What does the doctor say?"

"Same old thing," Maddy said, doing her best stuffy-surgeon impression, chin raised, nose in the air. "Medulloblastoma is a rare and aggressive brain cancer. Don't get your hopes up." Then, dropping the schtick, "'Don't get your hopes up?' How do I keep from doing that?"

"That's what I say, honey!" Carol responded.

"Good question," Jamie Lynn said at the same time.

Maddy busied herself putting her coat and purse away and getting out some files. "And Tyler's wish is coming up soon."

"That's right," Jamie Lynn remembered. "Aren't you going to Give Kids the World?"

"Right," Maddy answered. "We get to stay at the Village for a week. And if Ty feels like it, we can go to Universal Studios, Disney World, the works. Ty's gonna love it. So will Ben. For that matter, so will I."

"What's it cost?"

"It doesn't cost us a cent. Donors and corporate sponsors pay for everything. Sick kids and their families get a real vacation. Everybody who's there understands what Ty and other kids like him are going through. Nobody makes fun of them, nobody feels out of place. It's really incredible. But," Maddy concluded, "I'm afraid I've used up all my vacation and sick time."

"Don't you worry, honey, we've got you covered," Carol said, trading winks with Jamie Lynn.

"Really?"

"Really."

"How's the money holding out?" Jamie Lynn wondered.

"Money ... money ...," Maddy mused, tapping her forehead. "Yes, that word sounds vaguely familiar. So far so good. We pull a little bit from here, scrape up a little bit there. There's some left from Patrick's life insurance. A friend of ours from the soccer league is organizing a fundraiser, and our church has really stepped up, really helped us out."

Carol nodded her head knowingly. "God's gonna take care of you, Maddy. Count on it."

"You're right," Maddy agreed. "We're really blessed."

Maddy picked up a patient chart, then thought of something.

"Let me check on Ty before I get started." She reached for her cell phone. "You mind?"

"Go, baby," Carol said. Maddy went around the corner to find a quiet spot to talk.

"You call that blessed?" Jamie Lynn demanded Carol once Maddy was out of earshot. "C'mon. First the poor woman's husband is killed in a car wreck, and now her son's fighting for his life. That's not blessed in my book."

"Maybe you're not reading the right book!" Carol declared. "Every day on God's earth with the people we love is a blessing. And if the good Lord takes that boy, he's going to take care of her too."

"That all sounds great, but I don't get it. How do you—"

"That's right, you don't get it," Carol said. "Girl, you got a lot to learn about life."

Granna had never given Ty his Heparin before. She was a little nervous but tried her best not to show it. Ty lay on his bed with his shirt pulled up, exposing a big gauze pad taped to the middle of his chest. Two surgical lines ran out from the center of the pad, and Granna was drawing Heparin out of a bottle into a syringe to insert into one of the lines. The medicine helped prevent post-surgical blood clots that could cause a stroke.

Try as she might, she couldn't fool Tyler, a seasoned veteran of the process, into thinking she was calm. "Are you sure you're okay doing this, Granna?" he asked.

"Nothing to it, kiddo," she answered breezily. "Your mom taught me, remember?"

The phone rang down the hall, further jangling Granna's nerves.

"Uh, Granna, are you absolutely positively sure you know how to do this?"

"Cool it. You're making me nervous."

"*I'm* making *you* nervous?"

"Ty!" Ben yelled. "Mom's on the phone. She wants to talk to you."

"He's in here and he's busy!" Granna yelled back without looking up, deep in concentration.

"Granna?"

She jumped. "What!"

"I've watched Mom do this about a thousand times, and you're supposed to wipe the ends of the tubes with an alcohol pad."

"Wipe the ends with an alcohol pad. I knew that." She grabbed a pad from the nightstand, tore it open, and wiped the ends of the tubing. "Am I prepped now, Dr. Doherty?"

"Yup," Tyler said. "Good to go." Granna connected the syringe to the tubing and started easing the medicine in. "Slow," Ty advised. "Make sure you don't get an air bubble in my heart."

Granna kept steady pressure on the syringe, focusing intently on her work. Looking at Ty, she saw his eyes widen. "Can you feel it go through?" His eyes were bugged out; his head quivered back and forth, and it looked like he was trying to say something.

"Tyler!" Granna said sharply, suddenly scared. "What's wrong?"

Ben stood leaning in the doorway, a portable phone in his hand. "Mom wants to talk to you, squirt." As he held out the phone, Ty let loose a bloodcurdling scream. Granna screamed. Ben screamed.

On the other end of the line, Maddy felt a tingle of fear up and down her spine. Something was wrong, and she wasn't there. "Mom! Ben!" she yelled into the phone. "What's going on? Somebody say something!" Then through the commotion she heard a cascade of laughter. It was Ty cackling with unbridled pleasure. "Ty? Ty! You rascal!"

Sitting on his bed, Granna gave Ty the sternest look a grandmother can. "That was not very funny, young man."

"Dude, you're such a jerk," Ben sneered, tossing the phone at him and slouching out of the room.

Ty was still laughing when Granna stiffened suddenly, grabbed her chest, then fell over on the bed. "Granna?" he called. "Granna! Are you okay? Granna, what's wrong?"

Granna popped up off the pillow and pointed at Ty with a mischievous smile. "Gotcha!"

"Mother!" Maddy hollered through the phone, still confused. "Mom, is everything all right? Do you need me?"

"Everything's fine," Granna said as the racket began to subside. "We're fine. Your son just has a warped sense of humor."

"Yeah!" Ty giggled.

"Don't you dare come home," Granna ordered. "We're fine. Just playing, if you can call it that, right, Tybo?"

"Stay at work, Mom," Ty called out. "We're just having fun." He started making gagging noises.

"Ty!" Granna called out, exasperated. "Stop it, you little stinker. Fool me once—" Ty leaned over and groped beside the bed for his bucket. He started to heave.

Watching him, Granna said into the phone, "Hold on a minute, dear. I think—"

Ty vomited into the bucket. On the next heave, he dropped the bucket, spilling its contents onto himself, the sheets, and the floor. And more kept coming.

"Oh, Tyler, honey, I'm so sorry. Maddy, we don't need you

here, but I'll have to call you back." Granna turned off the phone, set it on the nightstand, then rubbed her grandson's back as the retching continued. At the hospital Maddy clicked off her cell and said softly, "Okay. Call me back."

Granna helped Ty out of his soiled pajamas and changed the bed. As he settled himself again, she bundled up the fetid sheets and hurried down the hall to the laundry room, loaded the washing machine, then stood for a moment, drained, weary, rubbing her tired eyes.

"Is he okay?" She hadn't heard Ben come up, and she jumped a little.

"He's okay. How about you? You okay?"

"This whole thing stinks."

"I get that," Granna agreed. "You know, when I'm struggling with something, it helps me to pray about it."

"Pray?" Ben was equal parts incredulous and sarcastic. "What should we pray for, exactly? 'Dear God, please don't take Tyler. You've already got Dad. Isn't that enough?' "

Granna reached up and put a hand on Ben's shoulder. "If that's what you need to pray for, honey, then yes, pray for that. Prayer is just telling God what's in your heart and asking him to help you with it."

To her surprise, her words found their mark. Ben's eyes had been darting around, afraid to engage. Now he looked his grandmother in the eye. "I'm afraid to tell God what's in my heart," he said. "I'm afraid to ask God to help Tyler. Because what if he doesn't?" He paused, then looked down and shook his shaggy head. "Granna, I don't know how to do this." He shook his head again. "You pray. I don't know how to."

Granna took his hands and held them between hers in an attitude of prayer. Ben said, "I can't."

Granna kept hold of his hands, then leaned in toward him until their foreheads were touching. "Dear Heavenly Father," she said, "we're struggling here. We're scared and we need you to help us through this. Help Ben, Lord. He's mad about what's happening. He's mad because his father isn't around. He's mad because Ty is sick. He's mad because nothing ever seems normal any more. Help him feel your presence and know you're always with him. Help him know what questions to ask and how to listen for answers. Bring us rest and refreshment through the night and bless us tomorrow. In Jesus' name we pray, amen."

She hugged Ben and kissed his forehead. Ben hugged her back. She returned to Ty's room and found him lying in bed with his hands behind his head, looking out the window.

"Granna, am I ever going to get better?"

She sat down on the bed. "I pray for that every single night, sweetie, but only God knows for sure. But I do know this: he made one tough little cookie when he made you." Ty grinned and flexed his scrawny biceps. "Look out!" she pretended. "Here comes Mighty Muscle Man."

"Arrrgh!" exclaimed the seven-year-old superhero.

"How about a good-night prayer?"

"Okay."

Granna prayed, then kissed his bald head and left. As soon as she was safely out of the room, he got out of bed, grabbed his blanket, and climbed out onto his fort, grabbing a pad and pencil on his way. Settling himself outside in an old lawn chair, he looked up at the stars, thought for a minute, then started to write.

Dear God,

I puked all over the place tonight but I couldn't help it. I'm so glad Granna was here. How many people are there in heaven? It must be a lot. I know two and I'm only seven. Can you see the stars from there? My dad said you made them all. How is he doing? I'm really glad to be home from the hospital. I hope you get my letters.

Love,

Tyler

The morning sun beamed down upon the unshaven face of Brady McDaniels but failed to wake him. Between the shots at Jack's and the bottle in his apartment, he'd had more drinks last night than he could count. But he never counted anyway. His hair was a rat's nest, his clothes were wrinkled and stained, and the last bottle he'd drained was on the floor beside his recliner where he'd dropped it. A sound pierced the deep darkness of his stupor and stirred him slightly. He kept trying to ignore it, but the sound was insistent. He opened one eye and flinched at the sunlight. Then he noticed the blinking red light on his answering machine. But that thing didn't make a noise. The phone. It was the phone. With a great effort, he lurched his hand over to the receiver and picked it up.

"Yeah."

"McDaniels, have you lost your mind?" It was Lester Stevens, his boss at the post office. Lester's booming voice knifed through the alcoholic fog. "I leave you a message telling you to get your keister in here early, and not only are you not here early, you're not here at all. You are *late again*! If you're not standing in front of me in my office in thirty minutes—"

Brady picked his jacket up from the pile on the floor, raked his keys off the table, and sprinted toward his car. He was thirsty. He had to go to the bathroom. He couldn't remember if he had his wallet or not. But in his half-stupor, the only thing he knew for sure was that Mr. Stevens was on his tail and he'd better be at work pronto. Lester's voice continued pouring out of the phone into the empty room. "I am running out of patience. This is the sound of me running out of patience. My good humor will only stretch so far. There's a line of people a mile long who want this job, and today one of them just might get it. McDaniels, are you listening to me?"

Within minutes Brady had weaved and roared to the post office. He trotted in from the parking lot, tucking in his shirt and combing his hair with his fingers as he went. Walking quickly through the maze of work areas and hallways to Mr. Stevens's office, he rounded the corner through his doorway and found him seated behind his desk. Stevens looked up from a stack of papers and gave McDaniels the once-over.

"Did you sleep in that shirt?"

"No, sir, Mr. Stevens. It got wrinkled in the drawer."

Brady seemed a little unsteady on his feet. "You all right?"

"Yes, sir, ready to go out. Ready to go."

Lester handed him a card. Brady studied it, trying to make all the letters and words sit still. His head was pounding. Finally the marks on the card lined up for an instant. He looked at Lester, who was rising to his feet. "A walking route?"

Lester headed out the office door and motioned Brady to follow him. "A walking route. You know, one foot in front of the other. From point A to point B. Deliver the mail in between."

"If it's all the same to you," Brady said, "I'd rather stay on the sorting line. Really, Mr. Stevens, I can't do a walking route." He added to himself, *at least not today.*

Lester kept walking, and Brady stuck close behind him. "You can, and you will." He opened a wall cabinet and selected a set of keys. "Here are your keys. The truck is in twenty-seven, loaded and ready to go. Here's your route map. There's a clean uniform in the locker room. You're already two hours behind, so I'd step on it if I were you."

In a trancelike state, Brady walked toward the loading dock.

"Ben, get up. You're going to be late!" Maddy called from the bottom of the stairs.

"Chill out, Mom," came the distant reply from Ben's room. He was still in bed, as usual, and about to miss the school bus, as usual. On the days Maddy was home, she enjoyed fixing breakfast for the boys. She stepped back in front of the stove, where eggs sizzled in a skillet. Ty probably wouldn't go to school first thing this morning, though he might go later. She'd make him some toast when he got up. Ben was supposed to be at the bus stop in ten minutes, and it was anybody's guess whether he'd make it or not.

"I'm not driving you to school again," she called out. "You miss the bus, you walk."

"Then I'll stay home." Ben padded to the top of the stairs in a T-shirt and shorts. "I shouldn't have to take the bus anyway. I should have my driver's license like everybody else in the universe my age." Maddy had heard it all before. She went back toward the kitchen as Ben headed for the bathroom.

Ty lay in his bed dozing through all the commotion. But then he heard a familiar sound that made him open his eyes with a wide smile.

Tap, tap, tap! The sound of knocking on his bedroom window. Ty sat up. "Sam!" he said in an excited whisper.

Ty clambered out of bed, and with him pulling from inside and Sam helping from outside, they got the window up, and she stepped over the sill into his room. She wore a pink robe over pink pajamas, but the feminine effect was checked by her dark brown hair tucked under a baseball cap, which she wore backward, and a pair of rubber boots.

"It's about time!" Sam scolded playfully. "I've been tapping for an hour. Mom told me you got back, but she wouldn't let me come over till later. I figured this was later. How do you feel? Are you better?"

"Working on it," Ty said with enthusiasm.

"Let me look at you."

Tyler stood tall, ready for inspection and flashing a toothy grin. But he felt a chill, crumpled onto the bed, and wrapped himself in the covers. Sam closed the window.

She took in his bald head, with its precise scar up the back, and his pale complexion. "You don't look so bad," she lied.

"I feel lots better," he lied. "I think I'm going back to school even."

"Thank goodness!" Sam said happily. "If I have to eat lunch one more day with Ashley Turner, I'll just die. It's horrible. She smells like liverwurst."

"Eeeewww," Tyler said.

"'Eeeewww' is right," Sam agreed. "Here, I got you this." She reached inside her robe and pulled out a bright green knit cap, positioning it on Ty's head.

"Sweet! Thanks!" Tyler said, reaching up to feel the cap and admiring it in the mirror above his dresser.

He heard footsteps. "Quick! My mom's coming!" Sam dove

under the bed just as Maddy walked in. She was surprised to see her son up.

"Hey, Tybo, you're awake."

"Yep, I'm awake all right," Ty said self-consciously. "Just lying here being awake."

Maddy noticed the window wasn't shut all the way. She'd checked it herself last night, and as cold-natured as Ty was these days, he wouldn't have thought about opening it. She also didn't remember seeing that knit cap before. She raised one eyebrow.

"New hat?"

Ty's eyes widened as he snatched the cap off his head and buried it under the covers. "What, this thing?" he asked, then quickly changed the subject. "So, I'm going to school today, right?"

"You feel up to it?"

"Yeah, I think so."

His mother felt his forehead. As she leaned over, she noticed a pair of boots—with legs attached—peeking out from under the bed. "I don't know. What do you think, Sam?"

A muffled giggle came from under the bed. "I think he's ready," said a disembodied voice.

"Way to go, Sam!" Ty said. The jig was up.

Sam peeked up over the bed. "Hi, Miss Maddy."

"Hi, Samantha," Maddy answered. "How are you?"

"I'm fine. Mom told me Tyler was home. I just wanted to come over and say 'welcome back.'"

Maddy crossed her arms and looked back and forth from one kid to the other. Ty was sure lucky to have a friend like Sam. He was going to need some good friends. She pointed at Ty. "Well, if you're going to school, I guess you'd better start getting ready."

Ty climbed out of bed as Sam headed for the window. "Sam!" Maddy called. "Front door, please."

"Oh, sure, Miss Maddy. See you at the bus, Ty."

"Sam, I'll have to check him in at school. He'll catch up with you later. Now scoot!"

"Yes, ma'am." She took off down the hall, passing Ben on his way downstairs, who stared at her without speaking. Sam went out the front door, and Ben plopped down at the kitchen table, where Granna was just serving up a plate of scrambled eggs. He shoved away from the table, got a carton of orange juice out of the refrigerator, and filled his glass. As he sat back down, sullen and half-asleep, the school bus horn blared. With a grimace, he shoveled in a few forkfuls of eggs, grabbed his backpack, and ran out the back door.

Upstairs, Ty finished dressing and stood in front of his mirror looking at his bald head. Maddy sat on the bed watching him. She handed him his new cap. "Mom, do you think the kids will make fun of me?"

"Some of them will, because they don't know what else to say."

"What should I do if they do?" Maddy was still thinking how to answer when Ty beat her to it. "I know. I'll do what Jesus would do."

His words momentarily startled her. Looking at her son's pale, thin body and shiny head, she found it hard sometimes to accept the fact that Jesus had any part in all this.

"What would Jesus do, you think?" she asked.

"He would be kind and understanding and give them some slack."

She still fretted about sending him back to school. Maybe he should wait another day or two. "You know, you don't have to go today."

"No, I have to go," Ty declared with conviction. "Sam needs me. Ashley Turner smells like liverwurst."

Maddy grabbed his shoulders and turned him to her. "I'm proud of you, Tybo." She pulled off his cap, kissed him on the head, pulled the cap back into place, and left the room.

Ty followed her toward the door, then turned back to his desk. He opened the drawer and took out a letter already addressed and stamped. He'd make sure to put it in the mailbox on the way to the car.

A Very Good Day

Miss Holley's second grade class had worked hard on the banner that they were now unrolling and thumb-tacking to the wall. "Welcome Back Tyler!" it said, each letter a different bold acrylic color painted by a different classmate, with the rest of the space covered in drawings, get-well messages, and autographs. Miss Holley was young—four years out of college with her elementary education degree—and normally bubbling over with energy and enthusiasm that rivaled her students'. Today she was nervous. Tyler Doherty was coming back to class after six weeks of cancer treatment. How would he look? How would he feel? How would the other kids react? He would be there any moment, and she wondered how the first crucial minutes would go.

"Tyler's coming back this morning, and I know we'll all be happy to see him again," she said, walking back and forth slowly in front of her twenty-five young charges. "You've done a fantastic job with the banner, and he's going to love it."

A hand went up. It was Alex, the kind of overloud, overconfident know-it-all that every classroom seems to have.

"Yes, Alex?"

"Like, can I catch his disease? You know, if he spits on me or something?"

Before Miss Holley could answer, Samantha turned around

and took matters into her own hands. "No, you knucklehead! He has cancer, not cooties!"

The room tittered with laughter. Miss Holley fought for self-control, limiting her reaction to a barely noticeable upturn of the corners of her mouth. "Samantha," she scolded, though her heart wasn't in it, "we don't call people names." She turned to Alex. "No, Alex, cancer is not contagious." She took a step back to include the whole room. "Tyler has been through a lot. He's missed over a month of school, so he's going to feel a little weird, a little scared at first. He may look different than the last time you saw him and feel embarrassed about that. So let's all welcome him back to class with big smiles, hugs, and," looking directly at Alex, "kind words."

Miss Holley glanced at her watch. "All right then, while we wait for him, I need everyone to open your math workbooks to page twenty-one." With a chorus of groans, the children fished around under their desks for their materials.

It was after eleven when Ty and his mother pulled into the school parking lot. To Ty it seemed like everything that morning had taken forever to do—eating, loading his backpack, even walking out to the car and riding through the neighborhood. But he was too excited even to dream of staying home.

Maddy looked at her son. She was so proud of him. "Do you want me to walk in with you?"

Ty smiled. "I don't mind." He touched the knit cap on his head.

"Good. It'd be too bad if you did." She touched his nose with her forefinger.

"Look, it's Tyler! He's back!" Two girls walking by waved frantically through the window of the van. "Hey, Tyler!"

Eyes wide, mouth open, Ty looked pleadingly at his mom.

"Go on. I'll catch up," she said. He jumped out of the van. "Lord, give him strength," she said under her breath. "Give us both strength."

By the time she got to the attendance office to sign him in, he'd already headed for his classroom. "He was so excited, I let him go on," the attendance clerk, Mrs. Williams, said. "I told him he could talk in the hall, but to wait for you before he went to class. I figured you'd want to say bye and wish him luck." She gave Maddy a mom-to-mom wink.

"Thanks," Maddy said. In the distance, she saw Ty standing in the hall talking to the two girls from the parking lot.

The kids interrupted their conversation as Maddy approached. "Hey, Mrs. Doherty. We were just talking about how cool Ty looks," one of the girls volunteered. "Yeah," said the other, "the shaved head thing is really in, and Ty's the only one at school who has it!" Ty blushed. Maddy felt encouraged.

As the girls went on their way, Maddy put her arm around Ty's shoulders. He felt so bony to her, yet straight and solid. "Ready?"

He took a deep breath. "Ready."

Maddy tapped at the classroom door. Miss Holley opened it, and Ty took a step inside while his mother hung back in the hall.

"One, two, three: *Welcome back, Tyler!*" the teacher said as the class joined in, then broke out in exuberant applause punctuated by shouts of "Hey, Tiger!" "We missed you so much!" "Way to go!" Sam got right up in his face. "It's about time!" she declared, scrunching up her nose at him.

As Ty was surrounded by his friends, Maddy and Miss Holley conferred in the doorway.

"We're so glad to see Tyler back," the teacher said. "Is there anything I should be on the lookout for?"

"Not really. Just that he may get tired. If he does, call me and I'll come pick him back up."

"Will do." Then to the class, "All right, it's time for lunch. Who's line leader today? Amy?"

Chattering and flitting like a flock of colorful birds, the kids started lining up. When Ty hesitated, Sam grabbed him by the arm. "C'mon. Have you forgotten how to have fun?" As they filed out toward the lunchroom, Ty flashed his mother the biggest smile imaginable. Her heart skipped a beat.

"I'll pay attention, Mrs. Doherty," Miss Holley was saying as the room emptied and she went to bring up the end of the line.

"He still has a central medicine line in his chest," Maddy called after her, "so he shouldn't go under water." Then she thought about what she'd just said. "Maddy, you're being a silly mom. He won't be going under water on the playground." She watched him till he turned the corner.

At Miss Holley's row of lunchroom tables, Ty Doherty was the star attraction. "I'm going back so they can give me medicine from a bag," he explained. "It makes me real sick. They do that for a while, then I get my cells back, and then I'm done."

"So you won't be here the rest of the school year?" asked Ashley Turner from a couple of seats down the way.

"Not full time, not for a while."

Alex stared theatrically at Ty's head. "Did they call you baldy? Is that why you wear this stupid hat?"

Ty looked surprised at the question, but Sam took it personally. "I'm warning you, Alex!" she said.

"I bet that radiation stuff hurts," Alex went on, "especially a little wimp like you. Too bad you're such a wimpling." He flexed his muscles but winced as Sam gave him a sharp kick under the table.

"I don't feel anything when they do the radiation," Ty replied. "I have to lie real still for like twenty minutes — it feels like twenty — while this big machine points at my head and my back."

"A big machine points at you?" Alex wondered, unimpressed. "You mean that's it?"

"I guess," Ty admitted.

"What do you mean, 'that's it,' mister macho?" Sam rose up out of her chair. "It's a huge laser beam just like in *Star Wars* that zaps all the cancer cells, right, Ty?"

"Yeah, I guess," Ty agreed. "The radiation kills the cancer cells in my brain and spinal fluid."

"Is that what makes you sick?" Ashley wanted to know.

Sam leaned into her. "Not as sick as your liverwurst makes me!" Ashley stuck her lower lip out.

"Not too sick," Ty said, "but I heard the doctor tell my mom I probably won't grow like I'm supposed to because of it."

"So you're going to stay looking like an alien?" Alex prodded Ty in the ribs.

"That's it!" Sam fumed. In a lightning stroke, she lunged over the table, put her hand behind Alex's head, and jammed his face into a big helping of mashed potatoes on his plate.

Everybody around the table fell completely silent. As Alex lifted his head, his face was covered with potatoes—chunks running down his cheeks, gravy dripping from his nose and chin. A wild cheer broke out as Alex bolted from his chair and started chasing Sam around the tables. A couple of other teachers rushed to help Miss Holley break up the scuffle, then marched them, and Ty too, for good measure, to the principal's office for a little chat. The principal called everybody's parents, and Ty, along with Samantha, got to go home early even though he felt fine. In fact, he felt fantastic.

≈

Brady McDaniels parked his truck at the end of Laurel Lane. It was his first day on a new route and he still smelled like a rabbit hutch. Still very hung over too. To ease his reentry into the real world, he brought a big cup of coffee along and took a quick pull as he parked his truck. He ran his fingers through his hair and slapped his face briskly. He was awake, he told himself, alert, and ready to make the swift completion of his appointed rounds. Hefting the mailbag to his shoulder, he walked to the box at 229 Laurel, the Miller house, gingerly stepping around half a dozen little sprinklers watering the flowers festooning the yard.

The next house had a charming white picket fence. Brady opened the gate with his shoulder, heading down the walk to the box at 231. He heard a low rumble—a very low, very serious rumble—followed by the sight of the biggest dog Brady McDaniels had ever seen, loping around the side of the house. Brady stopped, Rooster stopped, and the two of them looked each other over. The mailman was rooted in his tracks: he was every Great Dane's dream.

Rooster came flying in Brady's direction. McDaniels tried to yell, but the combination of surprise and hangover turned the sound into a girlish squeal. Instinctively clutching the mailbag, he sprinted for the gate, but Rooster caught him easily. The huge animal wasn't interested in attacking; he wanted to play. First he grabbed the strap of the mailbag in his teeth and yanked on it, then caught a shoe in midstride and taste-tested a postal service pants leg.

Brady squirmed loose, dived over the fence, tripped on one of the sprinklers next door, and sprawled on the wet grass, pelted with water from several directions at once. He scrambled to his feet in time to see Rooster bounding over the fence after him. Running full tilt, he made it back to his truck and slid the door shut with a wham. Rooster put both huge paws on the side window, alternately gnawing on the rear view mirror and barking with delight.

After Rooster got tired of the fun and went on his way, Brady gingerly opened his door and took stock of the situation. As fuzzy as his head was, he knew he must look a fright—wet and muddy, his uniform torn—but he wasn't going to blow this chance. He shouldered his bag again and headed toward the next house, 244. In the box waiting for him were two letters, stamped and addressed to "God." Preoccupied with his recent escape, he put them in his bag without paying them any attention and turned to go.

"Walter, how about some tea?" He spun around and found himself facing a cheery woman with a bright smile holding a tall glass of iced tea. Seeing him, she started. "Oh my, you're not Walter."

"No, ma'am," Brady answered. "Walter's on a well-deserved extended vacation. I'm Brady McDaniels."

"Well, Brady McDaniels," Granna mused, looking at the glass and then back at the stranger, "I hate to see it go to waste." She gestured with the tea. "It's apple cinnamon spice."

Self-conscious about his appearance, he nevertheless took the glass and drank several long, refreshing swallows. It was very good tea.

"Wow. Is this stuff legal?"

"I believe it is," Granna said, beaming, "at least in most states."

Brady downed the rest of the tea. "Thanks a lot. I really appreciate it."

"You're welcome."

As Brady turned again to leave, a blue van pulled up in the

drive with a woman and two children inside. A boy got out and sped toward him, very excited, like he was expecting something. "Hey!" the boy started out, but before he could say another word he stopped in front of Brady, doubled over, and threw up on his uniform shoes. "Sorry," he said weakly as his mother led him inside.

"That's okay," Brady said to no one in particular, watching them go. "Happens all the time."

At the end of the day, Brady McDaniels wearily hefted his mailbag and dragged himself into the post office. Lester Stevens saw him come in. "How was it?" he asked. "You look like you've been mud wrestling."

"How was it?" Brady repeated. "The mud was the easy part. That's how it was. I almost got eaten by a horse and drowned by an army of sprinklers, and some kid barfed on my shoes."

"So that's what stinks."

As they talked, Brady walked to the sorting bin and started unloading his mail. He picked up the envelopes addressed to God. "To God." He waved them at Lester, then looked at them again. "I think these are from the kid who tossed his cookies on my shoes. To God. No zip code."

"If you'd gotten back on time there'd be a dead letter bin here, but at six it goes to the main office."

"So what do I do with these?"

"It's your job, Brady. You deliver them."

"Thanks for the help," Brady said gruffly, stalking off.

≈

Wrapped in a blanket, Ty sat in his fort, writing. It had been quite a day.

Dear God,

My first day back at school was very exciting. Alex started picking on me and Sam came to help. I forgot to tell her to do what Jesus would do, and we all ended up in the principal's office. Mom came to pick up Sam and me. On the way home she tried to be very firm, but when Sam told her how potatoes were stuck up Alex's nose she laughed and laughed. Now I know you're getting my letters, because only you could figure out how to make her laugh. She even laughed again later when I puked on the mailman's shoes. It was a very good day.

Love,

Tyler

In another part of town at about the same time, Brady sat on his usual stool at Jack's, draining his third or fourth or fifth bourbon. He watched Jack walk by one of the tables and ask the familiar, "Ready or steady?"

"We're steady," one of the guys said. "Thanks, Jack."

As Jack came around the bar, Brady shoved his glass forward. "Ready!" he declared. "Ready, Jack."

Jack gestured toward the TV with his bar towel. "Some game, huh? We're on a roll to the playoffs."

"Hey," Brady said sharply, "something happen to your hearing? Ready, ready, ready. Fill 'er up." He banged his empty glass harder on the table.

"Brady, I think you've had enough. And when I think you've had enough, you've had enough."

"Well, then, I'll just have to take my business somewhere else," Brady said with drunken indignation. "You're a royal pain anyway." He stood up, felt the blood pounding in his head, and took a wobbly path toward the door, steadying himself on tables as he went.

Jack walked out from around the bar and intercepted him. "Tell you what. I'll pour you one more." Brady looked at him, hopeful. "I'll pour you one more if you'll give me your keys."

The very idea made Brady indignant. "I don't see you taking anybody else's keys."

"I don't see anybody else staggering around," Jack said firmly. He planted his feet, standing between Brady and the door. "You can stay or you can leave. Either way, I'm taking your keys." He held out his hand.

Brady plopped down in the nearest chair, his head bobbing, trying to collect his thoughts. "If you weren't so old . . ." His voice trailed off.

"Keys."

Pawing through his uniform to find his keys, Brady came upon the letters to God and tossed them on the table. With a huff, Brady fished out his keys and handed them over. Jack brought him one more drink.

Seeing a child's handwriting, Jack picked up the top envelope. "Is this from your kid?"

"Some kid on my route," Brady answered. "We got a stack of these and I don't know what to do with them."

Jack noticed the address. "How are you going to deliver 'em?" he wondered with a laugh.

Brady shoved the letters back in his pocket. "Seems kind of wrong to shred 'em."

"If they're letters to God, maybe you should take 'em to a church." By the way he said it, it was hard to tell if he was serious or not. Jack wasn't a church-going kind of guy.

Brady had never thought of that, however, and it was actually a pretty good idea. Besides, it would give him a way to get rid of all those letters with a clean conscience. "I see your point, Jack old buddy. And since I'm hoofing it anyway, I'll see if I can find a church on the way. Wonder if God's at home this time of night?"

"Beats me."

Brady got up. "Okay, we'll see."

Brady stumbled down the sidewalk toward his apartment. He couldn't remember seeing a church between Jack's and home, but honestly, he'd never been looking for one. The longer he walked, the more he was convinced he was out of luck. Then, before he realized it, he was standing directly in front of one. It was scaled for the neighborhood, not too big or grand, but with a simple steeple on top and a few lights glowing inside. He felt the letters in his coat pocket and decided to try the front doors. To his surprise, they were unlocked.

No one seemed to be inside. He felt awkward in this unfamiliar place, more aware than ever of his torn and dirty uniform, even though he was alone. Soft light shone on the carefully waxed pews; the smell of wax hung in the air. There was a table near the door, and he put the letters to God there. Surely somebody would see them. He made a little stack of them at first, but that didn't look right, so he arranged them in a row. Still dissatisfied, Brady picked them back up and walked a few steps down the aisle. He balanced them on the armrest of a pew. They couldn't miss them there. But a gust of wind from the open door might knock them off. He laid them on a pew cushion. Maybe he should leave them more in the middle of the room. He tried a different pew, but something still wasn't right. Looking down the aisle toward the front of the church, he had an idea: these letters ought to be front and center on the table up there. He placed the letters down carefully and stood there with his hand on them.

"Can I help you?"

Brady jumped and whirled around. Three feet away stood a sandy-haired man about his own age. He had a kind, open face and eyes that sparkled even in the dim light.

"Hey, buddy, a little warning next time would be nice," he said curtly to the stranger. Then he remembered where he was. "I mean, you ... you startled me, sir. Reverend ..."

"Call me Andy. And you are ... ?"

"Brady McDaniels." He held up the letters. "I was just dropping these off."

The pastor stepped forward to take the letters and got a waft of liquor smell. What had happened to this guy? His clothes were a muddy mess; he was sloshed, stinky, and looked like some deranged refugee from a comedy sketch: a drunk and deluded mailman delivering letters in the middle of the night.

Brady watched as the pastor sized him up. "I wasn't stealing anything, I swear." He grimaced at his own statement. "Sorry. Bad choice of words. Let me start over. I came in because I think this kid on my route is writing letters to God, and I thought I'd ... that is ... I thought maybe here would be ..." He paused again "... I thought these would be better off with you, because honestly they'll just go into the dead letter bin and get shredded. At least here maybe you can ... I don't know ... read them, send this kid a gift basket or something."

Glancing through the envelopes, Pastor Andy noticed that a couple of them had "From Tyler" in the corner, and smiled. "That's very kind of you, Brady, going out of your way to make sure Tyler's letters are taken care of somehow."

"You know him?" Brady asked, surprised.

"We love that family," he said warmly. "They've been members here for a while. They've been through a lot, and it's tough for the mother to make ends meet. We pitch in and help them with little things here and there, keep them in our prayers, and check on them every few days." He studied Brady, who shifted his weight uncomfortably from one foot to the other. "It seems to me God put these letters in your hand for a reason. Maybe you should hang onto them." He handed them back.

"But Andy," Brady protested, with a tinge of alcoholic despair, "I don't know what to do with them."

"The first thing you need to do is go home and sleep it off." The pastor gave Brady a look. "Then, listen to God. Let him tell you what to do with the letters. After all, they're written to him." He waited to let that sink in. "And I hope you'll come visit us here again. You're always welcome. This is a great place to find answers."

Brady stuffed the letters back in his coat and started to leave but stumbled as he took the first step. Andy steadied him by the elbow. "Would it be okay if I pray for you and for the letters?"

"No, really, I'm fine." Brady pulled his elbow away with a subtle but definite move. "I'm good. I don't need your prayers. But thanks anyway."

God's Warrior

Granna was awake but enjoying that luxurious minute or two of lingering in the bed when it's quiet in the house, the birds are singing outside, and the day is filled with promise. Her eyes were closed as she listened to the sounds of the neighborhood coming to life and felt the breeze wafting in through the window.

If her eyes had been open, she would have seen a sneaky little hand reach up from beside the bed to a row of Styrofoam wig stands on the dresser, each topped with a wig and wearing a pair of sunglasses. Granna had a fairly impressive collection of both, and they were on private display in her room. Once the hand had snatched a wig, it came back for a pair of big Jackie O–style sunglasses. Then up over the edge of the bed came the face of Tyler Doherty, topped with a curly brunette wig and all but hidden by the enormous sunglasses. For added effect, he'd covered his teeth with an orange peel.

Leaning forward, he put his face inches from Granna's. She sensed his presence. "Morning, sweetheart." Then she opened her eyes.

"Aahhheeeee!" she screamed. Ty rolled on the floor with orange slice–muffled laughter, holding his stomach.

"Tyler Doherty!" Granna exclaimed. She joined in the

laughter and grabbed a wig and sunglasses herself, jamming them down in a cockeyed way.

Ty was staying home today. After the excitement in the lunchroom and the trip to the principal's office, then getting sick on the new mailman's shoes, Maddy decided Ty had better slow down and take it easy for a day. Since Ben, Sam, and all his other friends were at school, that meant he spent the day on his own. It felt great to kick a soccer ball around the yard again. He watched his collection of sports videos for a while, then grabbed his treasure box and climbed out to his fort. This would be a good time to write a few more letters to God.

Dear God,

one of them said,

I didn't want to stay home at first, but it's been okay. I hope Alex and Sam get along better today. Help them both think about what Jesus would do and not get mad at each other. I played some soccer and it's going to take a while to get back in shape. Maybe Ben will help me practice. Thank you today for Granna. She's really special.

Love,

Tyler

At the head of Laurel Lane, Brady McDaniels was ready for his second day on the route, determined to learn from yesterday's mistakes. Topping his list was making friends with Rooster. He peeked over the hedge and scanned the Baker yard: no dog. He whistled, then rattled the gate latch; still no Rooster. Cautiously, he opened the gate and headed for the porch. At that instant, the front door opened and the giant dog came barreling down the steps toward him barking excitedly, tongue hanging out, legs going every direction at once.

Brady stopped in his tracks and braced for impact. Making her way through the door, a very pregnant Mrs. Baker shuffled out as fast as she was able. "Rooster!" she ordered. "Sit!" Improbably, the monstrous dog immediately obeyed, parking himself on the sidewalk and whining to take off again.

"You must be new," Mrs. Baker said. "I don't think we've met before." The dog scooted Brady's direction a step or two but didn't charge. Brady eyed him warily.

"I'm filling in for Mr. Finley a while," Brady explained.

"Is he all right?" she wondered with maternal concern.

"He's fine. He's on vacation." Brady noticed a casserole dish in her hands.

"Mr. Finley's a dear," she declared. "He helps me out a lot. I thought I'd send a spaghetti casserole over to the Dohertys. They're going through a rough time, you know, with Tyler being sick and all." The dog kept sidling in Brady's direction. "Rooster! I told you to sit!" He sat. "I'd take it myself, but I'm not getting around too well these days. Would you mind terribly?" She held up the casserole.

Brady looked at her, at the dish, at the dog, and back again. "Uhhh, sure, I think." He took a tentative step. Rooster whined and lay down. Brady stepped around him.

"Here you go." She handed it over. "Thank you so much." As he took it from her, she twitched and grabbed at her stomach. "Ooohhhh."

"Are you okay?"

"I think so. Just a little twinge. I'm not due for a month. I hope he'll wait till his daddy gets home." She turned to go back inside and gestured to her enormous dog. "Okay, Rooster, back in the house."

Heading for the gate, Brady said under his breath, "She's going to need a bigger house."

Next door at the Dohertys', he saw a boy sitting on the front stoop tossing a soccer ball listlessly into the air. One glance and he could tell this had to be the kid Mrs. Baker had referred to: blue-gray eyes, very pale, and with an angry scar up the back of his bald head. He was also the boy who had made such an impact on his shoes.

"Hey."

"Hey," Ty answered back.

"No school today?"

"No, my mom thought I ought to take it easy today."

Brady nodded his acknowledgment, then gestured with the casserole dish. "Is your mom home?"

"Nope, not right now. But my Granna's here." He shouted over his shoulder toward the front door. "Granna!" Ty looked up at the mailman. "Hey, I'm sorry about your shoes yesterday," he added ruefully.

"It's okay. Cujo down the street pretty much ruined them already."

"You mean Rooster? He's a big ol' teddy bear. You just gotta know what he likes."

Granna joined them out front. "Well, hello again," she said to Brady. "Nice to see you."

She held out her hand and Brady extended the casserole. "It's from down the street. The very pregnant lady with the very big dog."

"Linda Baker. She is such a sweetheart. Eight months and

counting. Her husband's a soldier overseas, but she's always thinking about other people." She looked down at Ty. "You ready to come in, Ty?"

"Can I wait for Sam? The school bus will be here any minute."

"Sure. But if you get too pooped, come on inside and call her later."

With one hand holding the casserole, Granna took the mail out of their box and traded it to Brady for the incoming. They both noticed a couple of letters to God. "Good to see you again, young man," Granna said to Brady. He tipped his hat, winked at Tyler, and turned to go. Remembering something, he turned back around.

"Hey, kid. You said you could help me with Rooster. Can you really do that?"

"Piece of cake," Ty declared. "I'll meet you over there tomorrow."

As Brady walked to the next house, the school bus pulled up and disgorged half a dozen kids, all talking at once and dispersing up and down the block. Samantha ran past Brady and sat down beside Ty. "What happened at school today?" he wanted to know. "Tell me everything."

"Alex and I both had to write 'I will not fight' five hundred times. And Alex also had to write 'I will not make fun of people.'"

Ty rubbed his face with his hands, then ran his fingers over his head with its jagged purple scar. "People are always going to make fun of me."

Sam considered that fact for a minute, then sat up straight. "I know who can help." She jumped to her feet. "Come on!" They ran to Sam's house where, right on schedule as she knew he would be, her grandfather was in the kitchen pouring up a glass of disgusting-looking green slimy liquid. Even though he was the oldest person

Sam had ever known, he still had a classic actor's profile, luxuriant white hair, and a rich baritone speaking voice. He wore dress slacks and a sleeveless cardigan.

"Hi, Grandpa," Sam piped.

"Hi, Mr. Perryfield," said Ty. The old man greeted them with a curt growl and kept concentrating on his glass. "Eewww. What's that?" Ty pointed at the green stuff.

"My daily elixir," Grandpa said.

"You've got to drink that stuff every day?" Ty asked, incredulous. "Barf!"

"Barf yourself, Mr. Doherty." He held his glass up to the light from the window as the children watched. "Doctor says drink it, so I drink it. Like it or not."

"That explains it," Ty whispered to Sam.

"Explains what?" Sam whispered back.

"I'd be grouchy too if I had to drink that goop!"

"Did you say something?" Grandpa demanded, glaring.

"Grandpa, we need your help," Sam said, completely unfazed and unafraid.

"Can't," Grandpa barked. "I'm busy."

"Grandpa, please! It's big-time!"

Her doe-eyed expression was irresistible even to a grouch. He looked at the two of them and set his glass in the sink. "Make it quick."

He waved them toward the study that was his own private domain, stuffed with knickknacks and mementoes; cluttered with photos, yellowed telegrams in inexpensive frames, newspaper clippings, several bulging scrapbooks scattered here and there, and dog-eared copies of *Playbill* on the magazine table beside his worn but still elegant leather armchair that nobody else — absolutely nobody — ever sat in.

Cornelius Perryfield had never been a household name, but his handsome face had appeared over the decades in fourteen movies and too many stage plays to count. After his wife died five years ago, he'd come to live here with his son's family on Laurel Lane. He wasn't a mean-spirited or angry person — he simply didn't care what other people thought about him and didn't take the time to cultivate relationships even with those he loved very much, like Sam.

"So what's the big problem?" he demanded once they were all seated.

"The kids at school are making fun of me," Ty explained, patting his bald head. "And kids are going to make fun of me forever."

"All the kids are making fun of you?" Grandpa queried.

"Well, mostly one kid, Alex."

Mr. Perryfield examined Ty like Sherlock Holmes looking for his first clue. Then he held up an index finger with a gesture that would have made Holmes proud. "Well, it shouldn't bother you," he declared. "They're just jealous, that's all."

"Jealous because all my hair fell out and my eyebrows disappeared?" Ty exclaimed.

Grandpa walked to a small curtained doorway near one corner of the study and pulled the curtain back slightly. "No," he answered with a flourish. "Jealous because you, Mr. Doherty, were chosen for the role of a lifetime." He paused for dramatic effect. "You have been handpicked by God!"

Sam and Ty looked at each other, then back at Grandpa.

"If you don't believe me, just ask Baron Dadooska. Baron Dadooska?" he called behind the dark crimson curtain. Then stronger: "Dadooska, you back there?" As his audience watched, wide-eyed and open-mouthed, he continued his conversation from behind the curtain. "Dadooska, there you are! Ah, here he is."

After another brief pause the children heard silly giggling behind the curtain, then the sound of a strange voice singing in a goofy fake-Russian accent. Seconds later, so suddenly that it made them both jump, the curtain opened, and there was Cornelius Perryfield in the character of the baron, wearing an outrageous curly wig and moustache. Sam and Ty squealed with delight.

The baron looked mysteriously around the room, then set his eyes on Ty. "Aha!" He pointed. "You're heem! You must be heem! The famous Tyler!"

Laughing, Ty was instantly caught up in the story. "Why am I famous?"

The baron picked up a big Bible from the bookcase and waved it at him. "Becauss God has chosen *you*—de sstrongesst, de ssmartesst, de wissesst—to ressseive diss honor."

"Honor?" Ty wanted to know. "Like a gold star at school, Mr. Perry—"

"Who iss thiss Misster Nobody? I am the great Baron Dadooska! And the baron ssayss no, iss not that kind of honor. Iss de honor of being one of God's *warriors*!"

"Wow!" Ty exclaimed, both mesmerized and blown away.

"I want to be a warrior too!" Sam shouted.

The baron leaned toward one member of his audience and spoke conspiratorially, holding the back of one hand up near his mouth. "According to your principal, Samantha, you need to be a little less warrior and a little more ..." he straightened up "... peacemaker."

Sam considered the possibility. "Samantha the peacemaker. That really doesn't sound as good as 'warrior,' but I'll give it a try."

"Goot," Baron Dadooska replied. "Now where wass I?"

"I'm a warrior!" Ty reminded him excitedly, striking his most formidable warrior pose.

"Ah yess. One of God's youngest warriors, handpicked for the role of a lifetime. And that means 'you can ride forth victoriously in truth, humility, and righteousness.' That makes you the most powerful of all. Dadooska is honored to know you!"

"Thank you," Ty said.

"You're velcome," the baron said, his accent sharpening briefly before once again turning serious. "When people see how brave and strong you are even though you're sick, it makes them look closer at their own lives. And people, well, sometimes people don't like what they see. They're jealous. The truth will hurt, so they'll take it out on you like Alex did." With a superb sense of timing, the baron waited for this to register. "But there is a glorious truth, the truth that you show them: God is truth. And it's your job as God's warrior to point them toward him, because by turning to him, they will find truth. And wouldn't that be an amazing victory?"

"I think so," Ty answered, still puzzling it over.

"I don't get it," Sam confessed.

"But I don't feel brave," Ty admitted. "And I don't look like a warrior." He rubbed the smooth arches where his eyebrows used to be.

The baron thought it over; then the light came on. "Aha! I have an idea!" Guiding Ty by the shoulders, he positioned him in a chair. A couple of minutes later, he handed Ty a mirror that Ty, the baron, and Sam all crowded around. "Drum roll, please!"

The baron's luxuriant moustache had been transformed into a pair of phenomenal eyebrows for Tyler. "Wiggle them," the baron ordered. "Now one at a time."

"What do you think?" Ty asked Sam.

"They're awesome!"

"Cool," Ty said.

"Now iss time to go," said the now moustacheless baron. "Dadooska is tired."

As the kids scrambled from the room, Ty turned around, ran back, and gave Grandpa a heartfelt hug. "Thanks for the eyebrows, Mr. Perryfield. And thanks for the stuff about being a warrior. You're right. I am pretty lucky."

"You're welcome," Grandpa replied, then grumped, "Now go. Get out of here before I make you drink my green goop."

Ty sprinted to catch up with Sam.

Good smells filled the kitchen as Granna opened the oven door and took out two cake layers done to perfection. Ben moped in and plopped down in a chair.

"I made your favorite," she announced, holding up the cakes on cooling racks.

"That's Ty's favorite."

"Of course," she said, pretending to catch herself. "Yours is carrot cake." No reaction. "No, wait, marble cake." Still nothing. "Black Forest? All right. Sorry. What do you say we blame it on premature senility?"

"It's okay," Ben muttered in a tone indicating the exact opposite. "Forget it. Whatever." He lurched out of the chair to leave.

Granna put her hand on his shoulder, pushed him back down, and handed him a bowl of frosting with a tablespoon in it. "Sit. Stir. Now tell me what's on your mind."

Ben's thoughts were so jumbled up and tightly packed, he couldn't say anything at first. At last: "Nothing. Everything."

"Well, that pretty much covers it."

Ben's mind began to unlimber. "I feel weird. About Ty, you know. What he's going through." He was digging deeper now. "All the attention he gets. I mean, I know that's totally stupid and selfish. I know. I tried praying. It didn't work. I hate it that he's sick. I want him to get better, but I don't know if that's for his sake or mine. And I hate myself when I think like that, Granna, I really do."

"We all hate that he's sick. And I think sometimes it's harder on us than it is on him. So go easy on yourself. You've got a lot on your plate these days. Cut yourself some slack. And while you're at it, cut God some slack too." She looked at him and saw she was connecting. "Remember Job? He had it all: a mansion, a limo, great family, cows out the wazoo. He had it knocked."

Ben grinned in spite of himself. "I remember enough to know he didn't have a limo."

"I'm modernizing. Anyway, Job was a big shot in his time and very faithful to God. But then the ugly red guy with the pitchfork and the big horns—let's call him Satan—made a bet with God that he could break Job. Satan said Job would lose his faith if all his stuff was taken away. So Job fell on hard times. Had his house foreclosed, his limo repossessed, got sores all over his body, even lost his children."

"I bet he was ticked," Ben said.

"He wanted to know what he'd done to make God mad at him. But instead of complaining, he praised God for what he had left."

"That's whack."

Granna wasn't exactly sure what "whack" was, but it obviously wasn't good. "It wasn't whack to Job. He said, 'Shall we accept good from God but not trouble?'"

"But why would God take him down like that on a bet?"

"Because God understood Job's faithfulness. Job trusted God to do what was best for him even if it seemed horrible from a human perspective. Job's faith wasn't in exchange for God's favor—which is the part Satan didn't understand—it was unconditional. And when Job stood fast in the face of all those bad things, God blessed him twice as much as he'd been blessed before. Twice the cows, two limos, the works."

She stopped to catch her breath and let all this percolate. "Be thankful for what you have, Ben. Celebrate it. Everybody goes through hard times. Don't take it out on yourself. Or on Ty or God or anybody else. Especially don't take it out on your mother."

Ben stopped stirring. "I just want normal, Granna. I want to do what other kids do." He was suddenly agitated. "Do you know how many times I've asked Mom to take me to get my driver's license? Do you have any idea?"

"Well, uh . . ."

"You can't count that high!" He was wound up now. "One day she's too busy. The next day she thinks I'm not ready yet. Or she hasn't got ten bucks for the test. We can't do anything because we never have any money, because Tyler is always sick or in the hospital."

"'Shall we accept good from God and not trouble?'"

"All we're getting is trouble," he snapped.

Maddy walked in, rifling through a folder of bills. Without looking up she asked, "Ben, did you take the trash out?"

Granna, seeing her daughter wasn't plugged in and fearful of losing the moment, spoke up. "Honey, we're talking here."

"That's not going to get the trash to the curb."

"Talking doesn't matter to her anymore," Ben said despairingly. "All she knows how to do is bark orders!"

Maddy looked up from the clutch of overdue bills. "Ben, don't talk to me like that. I'm your mother."

"I've got a great idea. I'll just stop talking. What's the use anyway? I'm practically invisible as it is."

"Benjamin!" Maddy scolded.

"I'm sick of it. It's always about Tyler. Tyler needs this, Tyler did that."

"Ben, I'm warning you." Maddy's back was up. Ben bowled on.

"All your time. All our money. Everything. All Tyler all the time. I hate him!"

Maddy saw a movement out of the corner of her eye. Ty had been standing around the corner, listening to every word. Now he flew down the hall and up the stairs. Ben saw him go.

"Ty, wait!" Ben yelled. "I didn't mean it! Ty!"

Ben charged after his brother, and Maddy started to follow them. Granna stopped her with a word. "Maddy! Let Ben handle this. You've done enough. They've got to work it out themselves."

Maddy bent down and covered her face with her hands. "I can't do this," she groaned. Yet in spite of her misery, a laugh started forming as her mind replayed the last few seconds. Even as the tears welled up, a smile broke across her face as she caught her mother's gaze.

"Were those *eyebrows?*" She let the laugh come on out.

Never Too Late

Ty retreated to his fort, and Ben came crawling out the window after him. His brother was the last person in the world Ty wanted to see right now.

"Go away or I'll jump," he threatened.

"No you won't."

"How do you know?"

"Because it took me a week to talk you into coming out here the first time." Ben wasn't sure what to say next but knew it had to be good. "Look, Ty, I'm sorry. I didn't mean that stuff. I was blowing off steam, that's all."

Ty's eyes drilled into his. "What do you see when you look at me?"

"What? Don't be—"

"I'm serious!" Ty didn't cry that much anymore, but frustration and confusion had him on the verge of tears. "I know you're mad at me because I'm sick. Well I can't help it!"

"I'm not mad at you and I don't hate you," Ben said. "I *miss* you! I miss you, Tybo. I miss the stuff we used to do together, and I'm afraid we'll never have the chance to do it again." As good as it felt to say those things, Ben sensed things were getting pretty deep. "You're such a dweeb."

"You're such a toad," Ty shot back. He fished through his

treasure box for a pencil and paper, then shoved them at Ben. "Here. I want you to write a letter to God."

"What?"

"Write a letter to God," Ty repeated. Ben looked unconvinced. "You need to at least try it. Tell him how you feel. Ask him your questions; ask him the hard stuff. I know he can help you and Mom."

"Tyler, that is *so* lame."

"It's not lame!" He thrust his face inches from Ben's. "It's my favorite way to talk to God. It was Dad's favorite way. It's how to find the truth."

Ben had no comeback. "Okay. All right." He took the pencil and paper. "I'll give it a whirl."

The two sat together and wrote as the sun set on Laurel Lane.

"I'm a warrior, you know," Ty said without looking up, writing intently.

"With those eyebrows, you're going to have to be."

Ty smiled. He was starting to fulfill his purpose, just like Baron Dadooska said.

By the time Brady McDaniels parked his mail truck at the end of the street the next day, Ty was already pacing up and down the sidewalk, waiting for him. Sam was there too, since she had no intention of missing out on the fun. Brady grabbed his big bag and joined them.

"Ready?" Ty asked.

"I guess," Brady said, not ready at all. They walked stealthily to the hedge around the Bakers' yard and raised their heads until there were six eyeballs in a line just above the carefully clipped shrubs. "You sure about this?" Brady asked warily.

"Works every time," Sam assured him.

Brady unscrewed the top from a jar of peanut butter, opened the gate, and whistled nervously. Rooster came galloping around the corner like a shot. Brady closed his eyes and braced for impact. Instead of jumping him, Rooster went for the jar and started licking furiously. Brady walked the rest of the way to the porch with the dog seemingly stuck to the jar, licking nonstop. Safely back outside the gate, Brady capped the jar. Licking the last bits off his nose, Rooster turned away and headed for the house calm and satisfied.

Brady and the kids walked toward the Doherty house. "Unbelievable," Brady declared with a smile and a shake of his head.

"Told ya," said Ty, dribbling a soccer ball with his hand as he went.

"Peanut butter cookies work in a pinch," Sam offered, "but you've got to have a bunch of them."

"You're supposed to kick that thing, Tiger." Brady gestured toward the ball.

"Hey, my dad used to call me that," Ty said, pleased.

"Well, I gotta go," Sam said. "Got to be home by three. Piano lessons." She made a sour face. "See ya, Ty. Bye, Mr. Brady."

"Hey Sam," Brady called, holding out a handful of mail, "would you mind? It'll spare your grandfather having to complain about me."

"Sure. But his bark is lots worse than his bite." She took the mail and ran toward home.

Brady and Ty continued down the sidewalk. "So is she your girlfriend?" Brady teased.

"Yuck! No way!"

"Sorry I asked."

"She's my best 'like-a-guy' friend. An actual friend who happens to be a girl."

"Gotcha."

As they turned the corner into Ty's yard, Brady dropped his bag, snatched the soccer ball out of Ty's hand, and started dribbling with his feet. Ty raced after him. Brady passed him the ball, then stole it. Ty stole it right back.

"Cool!" Ty exclaimed. "Do you have any kids?"

"I have a son a little younger than you. He lives with his mom, though, so I don't see him much." For a flash, Brady's son's face was where Ty's should have been.

"That's too bad."

Brady stole the ball from Ty and "bent" it like soccer superstar David Beckham, spinning it as he kicked to make it curve in the air. Now Ty was really impressed. With a move like that, he could score on a free kick every time.

"Wow! Hey, maybe you can teach me that move. After all, I saved your life."

Brady chuckled. "I guess you did. I would have been Rooster's hot snack today if it hadn't been for you. Say, Ty, you're good. Are you on a team?"

"Yeah, but I haven't played since I got sick. I sure miss it."

"In the meantime, you can practice this." He showed him the Beckham move, approaching the ball at an angle, then kicking it with the side of his toe to make it spin just right.

While the two of them were hard at work, Maddy came out and stood at the top of the porch steps. "Ty," she called, "go wash up. I'm leaving in a few minutes."

Brady and Ty stopped their practice and walked toward Maddy. "Thanks for the game," Ty said as he broke into a trot and headed inside.

"You bet, Tiger." Thinking of soccer with his dad made Ty happy. Brady stopped at the bottom of the steps. "Hi. I'm Brady." He extended his hand and Maddy shook it.

"Madalynn Doherty. Everybody calls me Maddy."

"I know." Maddy cocked her head in a way that said, *How do you know?* "I deliver your mail."

"Of course you do. Hence the uniform and the big bag full of mail."

Brady couldn't deny he felt a spark of something as he talked to Ty's friendly and attractive mother. For her part, Maddy had long since decided she was too busy and too emotionally fried to even think about personal relationships right now. But this man was so kind to Tyler; it was like he knew intuitively what her son needed. And rumpled as he was, he was definitely easy on the eyes. Brady noticed Ty watching them from his window.

"Right. Just filling in." Brady explained. He pondered whether to ask the next question. "He's going to be okay, isn't he? I mean, he's going to get well."

"We hope so."

"Good. Good. He's a good kid." She smiled and watched him as he turned to go. "Brady?" He turned back. She pointed to the mailbag in the yard where he'd dropped it to play.

"Oh, yeah. I'm gonna need that." He started off, then turned back a second time to hand Maddy her mail. "Here you go. I don't know where my head is today."

"That's okay." She rifled through the stack. "It's mostly bills anyway. Thanks for taking some time with Tyler. I could tell it meant a lot to him."

The sound of the phone ringing came from inside, then Ben shouting, "Mom, phone!" Maddy and Brady waved good-bye, and Brady disappeared around the corner.

"Mrs. Doherty, it's Dr. Rashaad." Maddy felt her stomach knotting. "I've been going over Ty's test results again and consulting with some of the other doctors here. I believe it would be best for Ty to start another round of treatment right away."

"That's too bad. We've just gotten settled at home, and he's only been back at school for one day."

"I know, I know. And under most circumstances, I'd say let's let him rest, let him go to school, let him be a kid for a while. But Mrs. Doherty, we don't have a while. I'm sorry to have to tell you that."

"Is Ty worse?"

"I'm not sure that's the right word. But we're at risk of losing the ground we've gained."

Maddy pressed her lips tightly together. She couldn't imagine the last seven weeks being for nothing. "All right. When do you want us?"

"Next week. You can go back to Memorial Medical, so at least it'll be close."

"Next week." How could she gear up for another round so soon? At the moment, she had no idea. "All right. We'll get ready."

She was supposed to leave for work but called in and said she'd be late, then went up to see Ty. Finding his room empty and the window open, she crawled out to the fort.

"Hey, Mom."

"Hi, sweetie. What are you doing?"

"Writing a letter to Alex."

"Alex from school?"

"Yeah. I want him to know I'm not mad at him and that I understand why he makes fun of me. Mr. Perryfield says it's because I'm God's warrior and I make him feel things he doesn't want to feel. But that's good because maybe he'll turn to God for the answers. Or something like that."

She was so proud of her Tybo. "Mr. Perryfield's a very smart man."

"So what's up? You're supposed to be at work. Why are you still here?"

"Well, honey, Dr. Rashaad called. It's time to go back and finish your medicine."

Tyler kept looking down at his letter. "Really?"

"Really." He looked up with fear in his face. Maddy reached across and rubbed his back, then hugged him tight.

"Okay," he said.

"Okay, Tiger."

At the end of the day Brady McDaniels went home thinking about Ty and Maddy and soccer and how those couple of minutes of playing had stirred up such vivid memories of playing with his own son, Justin. He carried his own mail inside and dropped it on one pile, then took the day's letter to God and added it to the growing stack Ty had written. What was he going to do with those?

One piece of his mail caught his eye. Tearing it open with a sense of apprehension, he could see it was a letter from his ex-wife's lawyer. Plowing through the legalese, he soon figured out she was suing him for full custody of their son. She was taking Justin away for good. Closing his eyes, he fell into his chair in shock. He had no idea how long it was before he finally got up and went outside to walk.

Ambling absentmindedly for a while, he realized he was standing in front of Jack's, and stopped on the sidewalk. Jack saw him through the window and motioned him in. Brady stood rooted to the spot. Jack opened the door.

"Hey, Brady. Brady?" He seemed to be in some sort of trance. "Brady, you coming in or what? The game's on. Come on in and watch."

"No thanks," Brady said with resolve. "See you later."

Deep in thought, he kept walking, paying no attention to where he was going. Looking up a few minutes later, he saw he'd stumbled onto the church where he'd talked with that pastor named Andy about Ty's letters. Opening the door, he heard music: Wednesday night choir rehearsal. A rich, powerful baritone voice was singing something about meeting Jesus. It sounded really good, Brady thought. He took a seat in the back row. Looking closer, he saw that the singer was Lester Stevens, his boss at the post office. That guy had a set of pipes! Brady had had no idea.

Listening to the words, he had a strange feeling that they were aimed right at him. There was a presence he couldn't describe that held him in his seat and made him listen. The music filled him up. Maybe this was what God was all about. Thoughts of his son, Justin, raced through his head, jumbled with bits and pieces of the encounters he'd had with Ty and his mother. And what about those letters to God? What was up with those? He felt a rush of emotion that was somehow alien and comforting at the same time. By the time the song was over, he felt as limp as a dishrag.

After rehearsal, the choir broke up, and Lester and his wife headed down the aisle toward where Brady sat. As he came close, Lester's eyes widened with recognition.

"McDaniels?"

"Mr. Stevens! I didn't know you went to church. Ah, I mean, went to church here. And what a voice!"

"Thanks. Good to see you here. This is my wife, Margaret."

Brady nodded hello. He didn't know what to say. Didn't know what he himself was thinking; didn't even know what he was doing there. "I, uh, well, you see, it's a funny story. I brought those letters to God here to drop them off. I figured the church could forward them to him, right?" He gave a nervous little laugh. "I was going to leave them, and the pastor said … well, to make a long story short, I still have them. And I thought maybe …"

His voice trailed off. He realized how completely stupid all this must sound. His thoughts were so mixed up there was no hope of making any sense of this jumbled monologue. He stared at his feet, then finally said softly, "It was nice meeting you, Margaret," and walked out.

With a knowing glance at his wife, Lester took off in pursuit. "Brady, wait up."

He caught up with McDaniels, and the two of them ambled slowly side by side through the church's lantern-lit garden in silence for a while.

"I'm a mess," Brady said at last.

Lester sat down on a bench. "You mind if we sit awhile? My mailman's knee is acting up."

"Sure, sure. You want me to bring you some water?"

Lester waved him over. "Just sit down a minute." Brady obliged. "You know, if you have something you need to work out in your life, this is the place to do it."

Brady thought it over. "It's too late for me."

"It's never too late for anybody, not when he's in charge." Lester pointed upward. "I sure don't have all the answers, but I'll help you if I can."

"But your knee hurts, and you've got to get back to Margaret."

"I don't have to get anywhere," he said. "And I'm sitting right here as long as you want to talk."

Brady sighed deeply. "Well, it's just that lately—" He corrected himself. "What am I saying? It's not lately, it's been going on for years. For years." He hesitated momentarily on the brink, then dove in.

"I just got a letter from my ex-wife's attorney," he said. "My son—" Brady looked at the ground then slowly back up, sighing deeply. "My son, Justin—still really young then—was riding with me. I drove past Jack's, where I, you know, run by for a cold one now and then. Jack's my buddy. I went in for one minute. One. Justin was asleep in the car seat, didn't even know I was gone. On the way home the cops stopped me. I failed the sobriety test, and they were putting me in the squad car and I said, 'Hey, what about my boy?' They took care of him until his mother could pick him up. Jack had always gotten me out of tight spots like that before, but this time, because I had Justin with me, he let me stew in the slammer.

"That was it as far as my wife was concerned. No more last chances. I failed at marriage, failed at being a father. Everything I touch, everything, turns to dust." Mr. Stevens gave him an encouraging nod. "It feels like everything's slipping through my fingers. I can't hold on to anything."

He paused, spent from the emotion of telling his story. "She wants to take my son away. He's slipping through. If I didn't have an incredibly understanding boss, I'd have probably let a really good job slip through as well."

"McDaniels," Lester instructed, "hold out your hands." Brady did so. "Now put them together and interlock the fingers." He looked at his hands clasped together, like he was praying. "Nothing can slip through now. Not when you pray. Not when you give your problems to God. You're right where you ought to be. Right in the palm of God's hand."

Brady nodded his understanding but unclasped his hands. He looked up at the night sky sprinkled with stars, then at the stained-glass window of the church glowing serenely across the courtyard. He put his hands back together and intertwined the fingers.

"Oh, Justin!" he said, barely above a whisper.

≈

At home on her couch that night, Maddy lay with her head in her mother's lap, spent, exhausted, a wad of tissues in her hand, her face red and swollen from crying.

"I can't lose him, Mom."

"I know, honey." Granna stroked her daughter's hair.

"It's so hard. I'll never make it through this."

"Yes, you will. We all will."

Maddy sat up and blew her nose. "With Patrick it was so sudden I never had time to react. I just kept moving forward because of the boys. I've always been the one who tells everybody else to be strong. Have faith. But look at me. I'm a mess."

"You're the strongest person I know," her mother reassured her. "You're a great mother. And you're not alone, Maddy. God has never left you, and he never will."

Trembling with emotion, Maddy struggled to her feet. "I know. Stay strong, Maddy," she mocked. "Trust God, Maddy. Whatever his will, Maddy. His will?! Well I don't happen to agree with his will! I have a little boy who's dying. Do you think Tyler goes along with God's will? Do you think he cares about that?"

"He seems to," Granna answered calmly. "He writes him letters all the time."

"I don't want to hear that," Maddy said, defeated. "I don't think God cares about any of this."

"Oh, sweetie, that's so far from the truth. God says—"

"Quit telling me what God says!" Maddy yelled. "Stop quoting the Bible to me. It's not curing my son!" She stalked out of the room.

Granna instinctively reached for her Bible, but put it back

down unopened. Instead, she turned to her desk, took out paper and a pencil, and started writing.

Dear God,

There's so much pain in my daughter's heart. She's moving away from you. Lord, that little boy needs to see her faith, her trust in you . . .

Upstairs, too engaged in their game to notice all the commotion, Ty and Sam sat on the floor playing checkers. Ben stuck his head in the door.

"Sam, your grandpa wants you home."

"Okay." She scrambled up from the floor and headed for her customary exit through the window. Halfway out, she stopped. "I'm sorry you have to go back to the hospital."

"Wait," Ty said, remembering. He pawed through his treasure box and pulled out an envelope. "Can you give this to Alex?"

Sam frowned and made a face like she'd just swallowed something awful. "Alex? You wrote him a letter?"

"Yeah. Just to let him know I'm not mad."

"Okay. But if he makes fun of it, I'm going to punch him."

"But Sam, you're—"

"I know," she interrupted. "The peacemaker." She took the letter and was gone. Outside, the roll of thunder announced an approaching storm.

Focus on the Good News

It rained all morning as Brady picked his way around the puddles on his way to the porch of 244 Laurel Lane. The van was gone and there were no lights on in the house. There was only one outgoing letter in the box, addressed to "God, Heaven on Earth," but it wasn't Ty's handwriting. Brady stared at the envelope. This was Olivia's—Granna's—writing. He walked to the door to knock, then changed his mind, slipped the letter into his uniform pocket, and continued on down the street.

Ty went back to the hospital for another round of chemotherapy and radiation to prepare for the stem cell infusion. The day of the procedure, Maddy was there, watching as the cells went in through the central line implanted in his chest, where the chemo was also administered. The whole process would take about three hours, so while Ty was dozing, Maddy stepped into the hall to stretch and almost ran into a familiar face.

"Jamie Lynn!"

"Hey, Maddy," Jamie Lynn said, giving her a hug. "Just came down to check on Ty. Us moms gotta stick together, you know."

"You're so sweet," Maddy replied. "He's asleep now."

"Has he been really sick?"

Maddy nodded. "Poor ol' Tybo. But what else can he do? The chemo prep makes him sick, the preservative in the stem cells makes him sick, and the follow-up medicine will make him sick. I'm surprised he hasn't thrown up his toenails."

"It happens to everybody going through this," Jamie Lynn said sympathetically. "Hard to imagine it's the *cure* for something. Goes to remind us all how tough cancer can be."

"He doesn't seem to be hurting any."

"That's good. He'll be nauseous and weak for a while, but then he'll start to feel all those healthy new cells bouncing around inside."

"I hope you're right."

The two of them walked into Ty's room. The door hadn't even closed behind them when it opened and, coffee in hand, Granna came into the room to take a shift sitting with Ty.

"Jamie Lynn," Granna said, "what are you doing on this floor?"

"Helping out," she explained. "This guy's my favorite patient, you know."

"He is pretty cute, isn't he?" Granna said with pride. "Hey, sweetie," she said to Maddy, "your relief is here." She held out the coffee.

"You sure you want to stay?"

"Sure I'm sure."

"I'll keep an eye on both of them," Jamie Lynn promised.

"Okay, you talked me into it."

Maddy wearily picked up her coat and purse and kissed her son on the forehead. He moved slightly and made a small sound, then sank back into a deep, drug-induced sleep.

"Okay," she said. "I could stand to get a few things done at the house. Couple of hours?" She and her mother traded kisses on the cheek.

"You take as long as you need," Granna told her.

The first thing Maddy wanted to know when she got to the house was where Ben was. Heaven only knew what he was up to. He was so complicated and difficult these days—as if her life wasn't complicated and difficult enough already. Looking around the living room, she saw signs of teenage-boy life: sneakers half under the couch; a backpack cracked open and its contents spilled out all around; schoolbooks, a video game controller, and a guitar all in a pile. Granna had gotten the laundry started: there was a stack of folded laundry on one end of the couch and a full basket of laundry beside it. Her eye caught a favorite picture of herself and Patrick on the table. She picked it up.

"We miss you," she said to the image in the frame. "But tell God he can't have him."

She showered and changed, then went to see what sort of shape Ben's room was in. He was supposed to be helping with the household chores, including keeping his room picked up and his laundry straight, but that wasn't happening much. Too tired even to think of arguing with him, she gathered up the clothes scattered around and reached over to at least smooth out his unmade bed. She wasn't going to make it for him, but she couldn't stand the pillows on the floor and the covers in such a mess.

The crackle of paper caught her attention. Tumbled up in the bedclothes was a wrinkled page covered in Ben's handwriting. She picked it up. "Dear God," it began. She sat down on the bed and continued reading.

I'm writing this because my brother asked me to. He's sick and I'm only doing it as a favor. He thinks it will help, but I don't see how. I've lost everything—all the big stuff when my dad died, and all the normal stuff with Tyler being sick—no hockey games, no concerts, no cookouts, no nothing. Why can't Ty get better? That would fix so many things. I know Mom loves me, but sometimes I think she wishes I was sick instead of Tyler. I don't blame her.

Overcome, Maddy pressed the letter to her heart. Ben was going through so much. Being sixteen was hard enough without all this other stress and hardship. She had a memory flash of him waiting for the school bus, towering above the other passengers, watching his friends drive by, some of them in cars of their own. A car was out of the question, but what did it cost to get him his license? Ten bucks?

She heard the door open downstairs. "Mom?" It was Ben. She stuffed the letter under the covers. He stomped up the stairs. "Mom?" Ben hadn't expected to see her at this time of day. "What's wrong? How's Tyler?"

"Follow me," she ordered, passing him and trooping downstairs. Entering the kitchen, she grabbed the spare set of car keys from a hook and hid them in her hand. Ben followed two steps behind her.

"What? What's happened? It is Ty?"

She tossed him the keys. He caught them reflexively. She said, "What's happened is, we're going to get your license. Right now."

Ben stood frozen in position. Maddy grabbed her purse and headed out. "Let's go, let's go!" she said over her shoulder. "I'm a busy woman."

As the truth dawned on him, Ben let out a war whoop, jumped into the air, and sped off after his mother.

At the Department of Motor Vehicles testing site, it was hard to tell who was more nervous: Maddy or Ben. She waited impatiently, nibbling on what little was left of her fingernails, while Ben went driving with the tester. When they returned, she watched as the tester tore a form off a pad and handed it to Ben, who was absolutely beaming. He walked quickly inside, waving the sheet as he passed.

"Hurry before they change their minds," she said. Inside, he filled out another form, smiled for his picture, and ran to meet her back in the parking lot, bouncing around like a big shaggy-haired puppy. "Hold still and let me see it," she begged as Ben continued his dance.

"I can drive!" he said slowly, still scarcely daring to believe it.

Maddy felt as happy as he did. "You can drive," she repeated. Then the reality hit home. "Yikes," she said, only half joking. "You can drive. Oh boy."

"Let's go show Ty," Ben said. "I'll drive. I said, 'I'll drive!'" It felt very good to say it. "Yes, thank you, I'll be glad to drive. Drive? Me? Glad to. No problem."

They got in the car, with Ben in the driver's seat, and headed to the hospital.

At school over the next few weeks, Tyler's classmates worked on ways to encourage him while he was sick and keep him connected with his friends. From Sam's perspective, one classmate in particular had really come around in a big way. She went to give Tyler the news, climbing up to his window and rapping as usual. "Hey, Ty, are you there? You'll never guess what happened," she said through the glass. "That God's warrior stuff must really work because Alex was nice to me today!" But there was no movement from the inside. Sam listened hard but heard nothing. "Ty? Tyler?"

"Sam, is that you?" It was Brady, down on the sidewalk.

"Oh, hey, Mr. Brady."

"Where's your buddy?"

"Must be at the hospital." She started shimmying down the ladder. "He needed some more medicine. I thought he'd be home by now, but it doesn't look like it."

"Too bad. Sorry to hear that." Sam jumped the rest of the way and landed in front of him. "Watch out there, missy. If you're not careful you'll end up in the hospital with him." He headed for the mailbox. "Did you knock on the door?"

She hadn't. But when she did, Granna opened the door. "Samantha! What a nice surprise!"

"Is Ty home yet?"

Granna wrapped her in a hug. "Not yet, sweetie. But I'm going to the hospital tomorrow, and I bet he'd love to see you. Wanna come?"

Brady handed over her mail and turned to go.

"And you too."

Brady looked back. "Me?"

"Yes, you. If you're 'Mr. Brady, that really cool mailman who plays soccer—he's *so* cool, Granna!' If you're that cool guy, I think he'd really like to see you too."

"I wouldn't dream of letting him down."

Maddy tried to concentrate on her magazine, but she kept stealing glances at Ty. Sitting in a wheelchair watching a video, he looked awful. Three weeks after his infusion, he was as pale as she'd ever seen him, with dark circles under his sunken eyes. Sometimes he was lively and energetic, but other times he became listless and unresponsive, like he couldn't hear you or didn't care what you said.

The door to the hospital room opened. She looked up, expecting her mother, but the face that came peeking around was Brady McDaniels'.

"Is this where they keep the soccer stars?" he asked as Granna followed him in.

"Brady!" Ty exclaimed, coming to life.

Maddy jumped to her feet and fluffed her hair self-consciously. "What a pleasant surprise."

"I have two more surprises," Brady announced. Motioning toward the door, he stepped aside as Sam walked in, wearing a dress, with her hair stylishly combed. Then came Alex, carrying a box of doughnuts.

"Hey, Sam," Ty said, brightening further. Then, "Alex?"

The two kids headed straight for Ty's wheelchair. Alex handed over the box. "These are for you and the other kids here."

Brady noticed Maddy staring at him. "Your mom invited me," he explained, a little self-conscious himself.

"I'm glad you came, uh, you know, for Tyler." She looked at Granna. "And Sam and," adding softly, "Alex?"

Granna took a step closer to Maddy and leaned in. "Alex's mom called last night. Something about a letter. She said he wanted to visit, so I said I'd bring him."

Sam wedged herself in beside Ty in the wheelchair, and Alex was pushing them around the room. "Mom, can I show them the play area?" Ty asked.

"I'll take them," Granna said to Maddy, with a wink to Brady. "Why don't the two of you go grab a cup of coffee?"

With the pride of a seasoned tour guide, Ty showed his friends the spacious play area around the corner from his room. There were platforms and stepping stones and a huge colorful pirate ship to climb on. Several kids were there, some of them bald like Ty, with a variety of bandages, scars, and tubes to mark their brave struggles against cancer. Alex found a spot near the back of the pirate ship and parked the chair. Sam leaned over to whisper something to Ty.

"Don't tell him, Sam!" Alex ordered.

"Come on!" Ty insisted, burning with curiosity.

"It's about your letters," Sam whispered. "Your letter to him gave him the idea. Alex got the whole class to write letters!"

"I'm warning you . . ." Alex grumbled, then changed his tone. In fact, he had a question for Ty, but it was so different from anything he'd ever asked anybody, he wasn't sure exactly how to do it. He'd been mean to Ty, but instead of being mean back, Ty had written him such a nice letter. Ty had something Alex didn't have, and Alex wanted to know more.

"So you know for sure you're going to heaven, right?" Alex asked. Ty nodded. "So how do I get to go?"

"Here's the thing," Ty explained. "You have to love God and be sorry for your sins. You pray, and you open your heart up to Jesus."

Alex looked confused. Sam said, "Let's try it!"

"I don't know how," Alex admitted.

"No problem," Ty said. "I'll pray out loud and you pray in your heart. But we have to hold hands." Making a face, Alex joined hands in a circle with the other two.

"Dear God," Ty prayed, "help Alex find the door in his heart and let you in. In Jesus' name, amen."

Alex tried it on skeptically. "That's it? I don't feel any different."

"I think it takes awhile to sink in," Ty said.

They were all still holding hands. Sam flashed a smile. "My family does this every night," she said. "It goes, 'I love you, squeeeeze!'" She raised her two hands, still holding one boy's hand in each, and squeezed.

The others mimicked her. "I love you, squeeze!" Realizing they were still holding hands with each other, the boys shook their hands away with a self-conscious giggle.

Watching from a chair across the way, Granna said aloud, "Lord, that must have been some letter."

When Maddy and Brady got back to Ty's room with their coffee, Dr. Rashaad was waiting for them. Maddy felt her shoulders tighten. Her mouth went dry.

"Dr. Rashaad, this is my friend—and Ty's friend—Brady McDaniels." She waited with tingles running up and down her spine for the doctor to speak. "Is everything okay?"

At that moment Granna and the kids came through the door from their excursion to the play area. Seeing the doctor, they stopped talking and looked at her anxiously.

"Well ..." Dr. Rashaad looked up from her clipboard and smiled from ear to ear. At her signal, a cluster of nurses, including Jamie Lynn, marched in with balloons and a sign reading, "No More Chemo."

"He's outta here!" the doctor announced. The nurses marched around the room chanting and throwing confetti while the children squealed with delight. As the celebration continued, the doctor motioned Maddy out into the hall.

"I have to be frank with you, Mrs. Doherty. This tumor is very—"

"Aggressive. I know. I know. But if he's finished with chemo that means he's in remission, right?"

"Loosely."

"Loosely? What does that mean exactly?"

"The MRI still shows spots on his brain, but I can't tell

whether the cells are alive, dead, or scar tissue. We'll just have to keep a close eye. For now, let's focus on the good news."

She patted her shoulder and walked off down the hall. Maddy turned back toward the celebration in Ty's room and gnawed on her fingernail.

Celebration

Brady McDaniels settled into the easy rhythm of his route, now greeting the homeowners on Laurel Lane by name. He sure hadn't wanted a walking route at first, but at this point he couldn't imagine spending his days back on the sorting line. Brady looked forward to seeing the people on his route every day and missed them when they weren't there. He said hello to Erin Miller, who was always so sweet but always asked when Mr. Finley would be coming back—not that Brady wasn't doing a fine job. Brady and Rooster had become best buddies. The monstrous dog never failed to greet him, and he never forgot his peanut butter.

Even Cornelius Perryfield had come around, grudgingly admitting that the McDaniels fellow was doing a passable job after all. One day as Brady came up the Perryfield walk, Sam and her grandpa were sitting on the porch playing checkers.

"Hey, Sam. Mr. Perryfield," Brady said. "Who's ahead?"

"I am, obviously," Sam said.

Grandpa reached over the board and jumped three pieces in a row. "I win."

"Hey," Sam blurted out, astonished. She hadn't seen it coming. Brady laughed and Samantha joined in. Even Mr. Perryfield cracked a smile.

"So Tyler's home and doing well?" Brady asked as he set the mail on a nearby table.

"Home," Grandpa answered, "but I think they're all going a little stir-crazy keeping an eye on him, watching for every little sign of improvement or trouble."

"They ought to do something fun," Sam suggested. "We all should. We ought to throw a welcome home party for Ty!"

"A costume party," Grandpa Perryfield said, as though the decision were already made. "Nothing more fun than a costume party." He picked up the mail and strode inside.

"You were right about the bark," Brady told Sam in a stage whisper. "He's a softy."

Once the idea got around, the party came together fast. Scarcely a week later, the Dohertys' front yard was festooned with fall decorations and ablaze with lights. Homemade signs, inside and out, welcomed Ty home. Granna had outdone herself, costumed as an Egyptian princess with gold and purple eye makeup and a dramatic foil headdress, while Maddy was decked out as a fairy godmother complete with wings and magic wand. There were action heroes and cartoon characters running everywhere. To no one's surprise, Ben came as Elvis, sporting slicked-back hair and massive sideburns down to his jaw.

As Jamie Lynn and Carol walked up, Granna intercepted them. "Hey, no fair," she scolded, pointing at their scrubs.

"What do you mean?" Carol demanded with mock seriousness. "We're disguised as nurses!"

"Where's Ty?" Jamie Lynn asked. Granna pointed across the yard.

"All I see is a tall Russian-looking guy," Carol said, still searching. It was, in fact, Baron Dadooska, with a long, elegant beard, huge bushy eyebrows, and an ancient velvet frock coat.

As the three ladies looked on, a miniature Dadooska peeked out from behind, identically dressed in every way, down to the bushy eyebrows. Two nurses and a princess howled with delight.

In the kitchen Maddy and Ben were loading up trays of munchies. She handed him a plate of caramel apples, pressed down his sideburns, and kissed his cheek. "This is going to be fun."

"Yes, it is."

In an hour the yard was packed with neighbors and friends: Sam was there as Pippi Longstocking, along with her parents, Tom and Liz, as pirates; Ben's friend Phoebe wore a poodle skirt and bobby socks; Pastor Andy held court as a jolly Abe Lincoln; Mrs. Baker had managed to shoehorn her pregnant self into a gigantic clown suit. Even Walter Finley was there: he and Erin Miller were outfitted as perfectly matched ketchup and mustard bottles.

Hours later, as the party wound down, Maddy sat with Brady, dressed as a cowboy riding a stuffed horse, on the front porch steps.

"This was such a great idea," Maddy said, tired but basking in the glow of a rousing success.

"It was all Mr. Perryfield's idea," Brady reminded her. "He really knows how to put on a show."

Maddy looked at the spectacle of Brady in that outfit. "Okay, I have to ask. Where did you get that costume?"

"I've had it a couple of years," Brady said, adjusting his mane. He paused; she waited. They exchanged a look. He went on. "My son had just turned three when I got home from Iraq. And my wife—now my ex-wife—told me his favorite animal was. . . ." He pointed to his costume. "So I ran out and bought this getup, thinking I'd be a big hero in his eyes."

"You freaked him out, didn't you?"

"Oh yeah. He screamed bloody murder for hours. Wouldn't come near me for days."

They shared a laugh. Brady looked over at Ben, who was tossing beanbags into a cardboard clown's mouth with Phoebe.

"Ben seems happier."

"Don't let that fool you. He's sixteen. Wait till tomorrow."

"Is he into soccer like Ty?"

"Oh, no." Sam, Ty, and Alex scampered by on their way inside, forcing Maddy and Brady to scoot closer together on the step. "He's all rock and roll. Or he used to be before Tybo got sick. These days he gets his musical jollies by wrangling the remote away from everybody else long enough to sneak a peek at the video countdowns. Anyway, he's had to deal with so much—his father's passing, Ty's cancer—way too much. And I was just making it worse with the driver's license thing and my whole attitude."

"I'm pretty good at making things worse myself." He shifted his position. "What turned it around?"

"I found a letter to God written by Ben. That's what it took to show me what I wasn't seeing."

Their conversation was interrupted by a commotion near the refreshment table. "Oooohhhh!" came a strange sound, followed by a groan. It was Mrs. Baker. She grabbed her stomach as two partygoers helped her to a chair.

Brady stared open-mouthed. "Is that what I think it is?"

"I think it's what you think," Maddy answered as the two of them headed in that direction.

"You know how to deliver babies, right?" he questioned hopefully. "Being a nurse and all? Because all I deliver is the mail."

"Calm down," she ordered, assuming nurse mode. "I'll get her into the car. You drive."

A knot of people were helping Mrs. Baker into the Doherty van as Brady opened the driver's side door. Sliding behind the wheel, he only got one leg in before his costume hung on the door frame. The horse head that stuck out in front of him wouldn't fit. Scrambling to get out of his suit, he got the ties knotted, then jammed the zipper. Mrs. Baker's groans were getting louder.

"Never mind," Maddy ordered. "Get back here with us. Ben!" she yelled across the yard. "You drive."

Patting his wallet with his newly minted license, Ben sprinted to the van, his Elvis medallion clanking on his chest as he ran. Brady and Maddy climbed in with Mrs. Baker, and off they sped. Ben could scarcely believe his good fortune. He'd had his license a week and every time his mother yelled, "Slower! Slower!" Mrs. Baker yelled, "Faster! Faster!" It was a dream come true.

Careening into the ambulance entrance, the blue minivan screeched to a halt. ER staffers who came out to meet them were momentarily floored to see Elvis at the wheel and a cowboy on a horse and a fairy godmother in back trying to help a groaning, panting clown through the sliding door. Quickly recovering, they hustled Mrs. Baker away. Everybody else went to the waiting room, where expectant dads must have thought they were hallucinating from lack of sleep.

After what seemed like only a few minutes, a nurse came to the door. "Is the Baker party here?" she asked. Cowpoke, Elvis, and the fairy jumped to their feet and followed her to the window of the newborn nursery. There were several babies on display; one had a name tag reading "Baker Boy."

"He's beautiful," Maddy said.

"He's all pink," Sam observed. She'd just come in.

"He looks like Yoda," Ben decided.

"He's here," said Ty simply.

It had been a very long, very exciting, very tiring day. It was way past bedtime when Tyler finally crawled under the covers and his mother tucked him in just the way he liked. She thought he looked very pale and spent. He still wore his massive Dadooska eyebrows.

"Want to put those awesome eyebrows in your treasure box?" Maddy asked.

"I'd rather wear them," Ty said, running his fingers over them. "They're my warrior brows."

"Okay, warrior. Go to sleep." She covered his face with little short kisses as they both giggled, then walked toward the door.

"Mom?"

She turned. "Yes, sweetie?"

"Do you think Mrs. Baker's baby was born to replace me?"

Maddy walked back and sat back down on the bed. "Why in the world would you think something like that?"

"Alex said Ashley Turner's sister told her that when someone dies, someone else is born to replace them."

She stroked his face. How she loved that face. "Tyler, first of all, you're not going to die. Not on my watch. Besides, I don't think it works that way. Nobody can replace you."

"But Ashley Turner's sister is *thirteen*!"

"Oh, she's thirteen. Well, with all due respect to Ashley Turner's sister, only God knows for sure how this stuff works."

Tyler yawned and burrowed deeper under the covers. "But if Ashley Turner's sister is right, I'd like Mrs. Baker's baby to replace me. He's really cute. And also, that way people won't forget me."

Maddy held his face in her hands and gave him an Eskimo kiss. "Nobody can ever replace you, and nobody will ever forget you."

Ty smiled and closed his eyes contentedly. Maddy straightened up and shifted her weight to stand.

"Mom?"

"Yes," she said, chuckling a little. Would this boy ever go to sleep?

"Tonight was really fun."

"Yes, it was. Really fun. Now sleep."

Meanwhile, down the street, the cowboy and his trusty horse had delivered Pippi Longstocking home to Baron Dadooska. Pippi was sound asleep, and the cowboy carried her in and put her on the sofa as Mr. Perryfield reemerged, carefully peeling off his beard.

Looking around the room, Brady was fascinated by the memorabilia. "Wow, you were in some amazing productions." He picked up a framed cast photo. "I remember this one."

He was interrupted by Ben's voice coming from outside. "Hey!" he heard Ben yell angrily. "What do you think you're doing?"

As Mr. Perryfield looked out the window, Brady headed for the door. He got outside just in time to see the Doherty's van winched up on the back of a tow truck.

Maddy ran into the yard, fairy wings askew. "Hey! What's going on? Who are you?"

"Sorry, lady," the driver said as he hit the gas. "This is what happens when you don't pay your bills."

"No!" She hurled a flowerpot at the departing truck. It fell short and shattered on the pavement. "Oh, that's perfect. Just perfect." Her laughter dissolved into sobs as she fell to her knees in the grass.

Brady stopped a step away. "It's okay," he said. "We can fix this." Maddy sat down, deep sobs wracking her whole body. He fished his car keys out from a pocket under his costume and jangled them.

"Here, take my car until we figure this out."

Maddy looked up. "I can't do that," she sniffed.

"Yes, you can!" Ben interjected.

"Decision made," Brady announced. He picked up a bicycle leaning against the porch. "Can I borrow this?" He heaved himself and his horse aboard and pedaled away. Maddy laughed in spite of herself.

Special Delivery

Maddy sat at her desk in the living room triaging the bills: this one had to be paid no matter what; that one she should get to as soon as she could; the next one would have to wait. Granna lounged in a chair across from her, reading a magazine. Ty was curled up on the couch, asleep, while Ben strummed his electric guitar with headphones plugged into it and scribbled fragments of music and lyrics on a pad.

Ty opened his eyes and Ben stopped playing. "Hey, don't stop," he said sleepily, "I like it."

"What do you know about music?" Ben teased, giving him a gentle poke. "Come on," he said, putting the guitar aside, "let's go kick it around."

Ty sat up stiffly. "Okay, but don't expect me to go easy on you." Ben got behind him and steered him outside by the shoulders. They started kicking Ty's soccer ball around in the front yard. Ty was game for action but slow to respond.

Maddy watched the boys through the window and began nibbling on her fingernail.

"Maddy!" Granna scolded, pointing to Maddy's hand at her mouth. Maddy jerked her hand away as Granna added, "I know that look. What is it?"

"I don't know," she said, watching Ty trying to keep up with his brother in the yard. "He doesn't seem to be bouncing back like he should. Maybe it's just taking a little longer this time." Now they were both chewing their fingernails. Simultaneously they saw each other and dropped their hands.

Glancing back out the window Granna saw Pastor Andy coming up the walk and waved him in. "Well, this is a pleasant surprise," she said.

"I was just down the street checking on Linda Baker and thought I'd see if you were home."

"How's Linda? And how's the baby?" Granna asked.

"Everybody's fine. She just got home this morning, and I think some of the ladies at church are going to check on her every day until her husband gets back. Shouldn't be long now."

"I know he can't wait to see his new son," Maddy said. "What did they name him?"

"I think I'll let them tell you themselves," he said mysteriously, then changed the subject. "By the way, I brought you something." He held up an envelope.

Maddy looked in the envelope, then reached for a wad of bills from the pile on her desk. "Pastor, I don't know how you and God do it, but you always seem to know what we need and when we need it most."

"I take no credit for this," he said, handing it over. "It's everybody. The whole church is behind you and praying for you." He headed for the door. "And by the way, you throw an awesome party."

"Thanks," Maddy said.

Halfway down the walk, he ducked barely in time to avoid getting smacked by the soccer ball Ben and Ty were kicking. Just then, Brady turned at the end of the walk and caught it. As they approached from opposite directions, Brady and Pastor Andy made a couple of quick moves on each other, then waved and went their separate ways.

Ty ran up, jumping with excitement. "Hey Brady, perfect timing. Show Ben that move you taught me." As Brady set down his bag, Maddy stepped out on the porch. "Tyler, phone," she called.

"For me?"

"It's Coach Dave."

Ty was off like a shot past his mother and into the house while Brady gave Ben his lesson. In seconds, Ty sprang back out. "Mom! Coach Dave wants to know if I can play tomorrow!"

The mother in her said no. He seemed so tired, so delicate. "Tyler, honey, I don't think you're strong enough yet."

"But I am! I am!"

Brady stepped forward to venture his own two cents' worth. "He sure looks strong enough to me."

"See?" Ty exclaimed.

Brady pressed on. "What's the worst that could happen? He gets tired and has to sit down."

"See?"

"I don't know," Maddy said hesitantly, her intuition nagging at her. "I really don't think it's a good idea. You haven't even been back to school yet."

"Please, oh please?" Ty begged.

"Please, oh please?" Brady repeated, mimicking Ty exactly.

Maddy glanced over at Ben. "I'm staying out of this," he said, holding up both hands.

"How about a compromise?" Brady proposed. "Ty dresses out, but plays only if he really feels like it and promises to take it easy. If he's not feeling so hot, he can help with the coaching." Maddy still resisted. "You gotta let him play. He's a natural."

Feeling outnumbered, Maddy gave in, in spite of herself. "Okay," she said finally to cheers all around.

≈

Back on the field! It was all Ty could think about the rest of the day. Next morning he was the first one up, had a light game-day breakfast, and was waiting in the car with his uniform on fifteen minutes before it was time to go.

The soccer field — or "pitch," as Coach Dave called it in his unmistakably British style — was in perfect shape, the weather cool and bright. The Tornadoes were there in a swirl of blue to take on the Riverview Red Dragons. Maddy had briefed the coach carefully on Ty's condition, and Ty sat out most of the first period, jumping out of his skin to get on the field. With five minutes to play in the game, the coach asked the referee to hold up for a minute and called his two best backs, John and Colt, over, along with Ty. Coach put his hands on his knees and leaned down toward Ty.

"Are you sure about this, Ty?" Coach Dave asked. Ty nodded vigorously. "I'm going to let you play goalie for the rest of the game. But if you can't get it, let it go. All right?"

"Okay, Coach," Ty said.

As Ty trotted off to the goalie box, Coach Dave put an arm around the shoulders of the other two boys. They were big and fast, and they loved their teammate Tyler.

"It's up to you two," he instructed them. "Whatever you do, protect Tyler. Got it?"

"Don't worry, Coach," John said. "No one's getting close."

"Not while we're back here," Colt promised.

"I'm serious," Coach Dave said sternly. "Anybody touches him, and you two mates spend all of next practice running laps."

As play resumed, Maddy couldn't bear to watch. She held her

hands in front of her face and peeked between her fingers. A big boy on the opposing team dribbled fast toward the goal Ty was defending. "Oh no. Oh, God, no," she muttered.

As Ty hunkered down to defend against the drive, Colt planted himself protectively in the challenger's path. "Get the ball!" Coach Dave screamed. "Get the ball!" The big Dragon blew right by, knocking Colt to the ground. John tried a slide tackle, missed, and went sprawling beside him.

"Get out of the way, Ty!" the coach roared. "Bloody move!"

The charging Red Dragon gave the ball a mighty kick. Ty leapt to intercept it, couldn't get all the way there, but deflected the shot with his fingertips. He fell to the ground, shook off the impact, then crawled on all fours toward the loose ball as the opposing player reared back to kick it again.

"Get out of there, Tyler!" the coach pleaded. Running toward the referee, he waved his hands and shouted, "Blow the whistle, ref! Blow the whistle!"

"Ball's still in play, Coach," the ref said, his eyes glued to the action.

The offensive player kicked again, hard, missing Ty's head by a whisker. Still on the ground, Ty blocked the ball with his body, then gathered it up into a fetal position.

Three whistle blasts signaled the end of the game.

Ty had saved the day. His teammates engulfed him, shouting out congratulations. Coach Dave was still upset. Yes, winning was important, but not worth risking a player's safety. "What on earth were you thinking?" he demanded, his words almost swallowed up in the commotion. "You could have really been hurt. But you did a fantastic job. Great." Sam rushed up from the bleachers, and so did Brady. Brady and Coach Dave lifted Ty into the air to the cheers of the crowd. Still nervous, Maddy pushed her way through the well-wishers to within earshot of her son.

"Are you okay?" she shouted up at him.

"I'm fine."

The men set him down and people surged forward. As Maddy watched, the big smile on Tyler's face turned into an odd open-mouthed expression. His eyelashes started to flutter and his head jerked back and forth.

"He's having a seizure!" Maddy called out. Tyler collapsed on the ground and lay absolutely still.

"Move back!" Coach Dave ordered. "Somebody call an ambulance!"

At the hospital, Maddy, Granna, Ben, and Brady stood in a semicircle around Ty's bed while Carol checked his IV lines and monitors.

"Mrs. Doherty?" She knew without looking up that it was Dr. Rashaad in the doorway. "Can we talk out in the hall?" She followed her with a vacant stare, arms wrapped tightly around herself.

"What is it?" she asked. "Did he overdo it?"

"This wasn't a result of overdoing it. Remember we talked about how aggressive this tumor is." Maddy closed her eyes. "We've done everything we can."

"Please don't tell me that."

"I wish there were something else. Anything else. He's a brave little boy. But we're out of options. I think it's time to send him home and make him as comfortable as possible. I do want to tell you this, though: he's no braver than you." She stared at the tops of her shoes. As many times as she'd done this, it never got any easier. "You'll be seeing a lot of me for a while. But I still want you to call me any time. Tyler can call me too." Dr. Rashaad pressed Maddy's hand between her own and turned away.

As the doctor left, Brady poked his head out of the room. He noticed the funny look in her eye. "Maddy?" he began tentatively.

She whirled on him. "Get out!" she exploded. "I knew something wasn't right! Why did you encourage him? Why did you talk me into letting him play? How dare you put my son's life in danger!"

Shocked and speechless, Brady kept listening as she ranted, but the words faded away. Suddenly he saw himself back on the street after his DUI arrest, and the voice he heard wasn't Maddy's; it was his ex-wife, Sarah's, terrified and furious: "How dare you put my son's life in danger like this? That's it. It's over. Go! Go away! Get out of here!"

Arriving back at his apartment, Brady headed straight for the freezer, where he kept an emergency bottle, just in case. He was so keyed up, so confused, so mad at himself, he knew a drink or two would help clear the cobwebs and straighten things out. He took the bottle into his living room and stood in the middle of the mess. The cold glass felt good as he touched the bottle to his forehead. In a few seconds, all the puzzle pieces would start falling into place.

His eyes fell on a framed photo of his son on the table behind a pile of Tyler's letters to God. God was taking that little boy Tyler away, but his own son, Justin, seemed just as gone. "What's the deal, God?" he growled. "What do you want from us? What do you want from me? How long do I have to keep paying?"

With a heart-wrenching sob, he flung the bottle, scattering the picture, letters, lamp, and telephone in every direction.

Losing control completely, he heaved a chair against the wall, crashed the lamp against the refrigerator, and threw all the books he could reach with both hands.

The momentum of his movement sent him to his knees on the floor. He realized he was on a heap of Ty's letters. "No, no, no," he said slowly, shaking his head. "I can't. Not now." He couldn't possibly read them. But he had to. Reluctantly, he sat back against the wall and opened the envelope on top.

Dear God,

I feel yucky today, but Sam really wants to climb trees. I already threw up three times this morning. Sam's going to need another friend you know. Better make it somebody who likes to climb trees. Her grandpa is lots of fun, but I don't think he can climb trees . . .

Brady finished the letter and picked up another one. And another. Silent tears tracked down his face and dripped on the paper.

. . . And God, please help me to tell Ben I broke his guitar strings. I didn't want to tell him, but I think he knows anyway. Help Ben forgive me. He's the best brother in the whole world even if he smells sometimes . . .

. . . I know it must be hard on Mrs. Baker. Babies cry A LOT. *She misses Mr. Baker a lot too. But she still finds time to make us good dinners and stuff. Don't tell Mom, but Mrs. Baker's fried chicken is way better . . .*

Some of the envelopes had drawings in them. There was one

of Ty and Ben playing soccer—two stick figures with a black-and-white ball between them. There were pictures: a soccer team photo, a school snapshot of Sam, a photocopy of an old family portrait with his dad in it. Movie ticket stubs, paper napkins from favorite restaurants, and other mementoes he'd included to help God understand the stories better.

> *. . . Mom came to pick up Sam and me. On the way home she tried to be very firm, but when Sam told her how potatoes were stuck up Alex's nose she laughed and laughed . . .*

Brady lost all track of time, drawn from one letter to the next as fast as he could get them open. The shadows grew long in his apartment and the sunlight began to fade. Brady clicked on the lamp that wasn't broken and kept reading.

> *. . . It's so cool that you're answering my letters. You know the kid who delivers pizza to our house that I told you about. He used to stare at me and look really scared. Now he gets so excited whenever he sees me and talks to me and tells me things. He even said he might want to be a doctor and help kids like me with cancer. Yep, you are so great! . . .*

> *. . . I think I'll be seeing you soon. I'm not feeling better like I used to. Before I die, I'm wondering if you can help my friend Mr. Brady. He is so cool and he has a boy, but I don't think they see each other. Just like me and my dad. But Mr. Brady lives closer to his boy. Could you tell Mr. Brady's heart that it's going to be okay? And tell him you love him. And his little boy does too.*

Brady felt waves of emotion washing over him: part love, part joy, part understanding, part thankfulness, part bittersweet memory. What treasures these letters were! He couldn't possibly keep them to himself. They weren't for him. But they'd be scrap paper at the post office, and Pastor Andy had said—what was it?—that they didn't belong at church and that if he listened, he'd know what to do with them. God would tell him.

As far as he knew, God had never said a word to him in his life. He and God were not exactly on speaking terms.

It was completely dark outside now, the light of the one working lamp shining feebly in the disheveled apartment with its smashed and jumbled furniture. Brady sat calmly in the middle of it all, mindless of the mess, of the smell of the whiskey from the broken bottle, the dimness, the fact that he hadn't had any supper.

Hours rolled by undetected. "Talk to me, God," he whispered. "I'm listening." Crazy as it sounded, he felt sort of like the way he'd felt that Wednesday night listening to music and then in the courtyard with Mr. Stevens. It was dim and still then too, and his mind was specially tuned in somehow. He couldn't really put his finger on it. "I wonder if I ought to write a letter to God myself?" he mused. That didn't feel right. He wouldn't know where to start. He never wrote letters to anybody.

But he did deliver them.

Brady parked his bicycle in the churchyard and took the steps two at a time. Bursting into Pastor Andy's office, out of breath, he handed over a letter. "This one's for you," he said without further explanation. "This one's yours. She needs you."

As Brady bounded back down the steps, Pastor Andy took Granna's letter to God out of its envelope and read,

> *. . . Please, Lord, help my daughter find her way back to you. Open her eyes to your love. Bless her . . .*

Wheeling up to the Perryfield house, Brady surprised Mr. Perryfield sitting on the porch. "Great Caruso!" the old gentleman said. "What are you doing here this hour of the night?"

"It's not the regular mail," Brady said, running up to him. "Special delivery." He handed over an envelope and dashed off. Mr. Perryfield started reading and was soon fishing for the spotless monogrammed handkerchief he always carried in his right back pocket.

> *. . . It's so fun being your warrior. Mr. Perryfield was right. Is there anything you can do about that green goop? Can I wear my eyebrows in heaven? Sam is going to need another friend. Someone she can take care of and who likes to climb trees . . .*

Brady pedaled up to Mrs. Baker, pacing up and down on the porch with her newborn baby.

"Another special delivery for you," he said, smiling, handing her a letter, and quickly heading off. Linda Baker shifted the baby to the crook of her arm to unfold the page.

> *. . . Thank you for watching over Mr. Baker. He's going to love seeing his new little boy. Please take care of all the other soldiers and help the families who already have*

somebody up there with you. I know you're in control of everything, and we don't see the world the way you do. Please help us understand. When things look bad, please give us faith that you know what's best. That would pretty much solve everything.

Love,

Tyler

The Best Letter of All

Tyler lay wrapped in a blanket on the couch, watching TV, surrounded by familiar, comfortable things. Maddy was seldom more than a step away these days, with Granna not far behind. Maddy sat on the floor beside her weak, pale son, rubbing his legs. She herself showed the strain of her vigil: jumpy, tense, and with dark circles under her eyes.

Granna answered a knock at the door, and Sam and her grandpa came in. Sam carried a small box in her hands.

"Hi, honey," Maddy said, standing. "So you decided to use the door instead of the window this time?"

"Grandpa says it's not tree-climbing season. Roofs either."

"What have you got there?" she asked, pointing to the box.

Sam opened it and took out a blue and gold wristband. "We had them made," she said, beaming. "Blue for his favorite color and gold for kids' cancer." Maddy took one and held it up to the light. On it was inscribed, "John 3:16—Believe—Love, Tyler."

"I love them," Maddy exclaimed, her eyes filling with tears. "Thank you so much." She gave Sam a hug. Grandpa kissed her hand.

"Hey, Sam," Ty called weakly from his nest.

Sam bounded over and plopped down beside him. The contrast between them was stark as they lay side by side. She seemed so hearty, skin tanned and hair shining, her body constantly in motion. He was so brittle and pale; his skin looked like china, and every movement seemed an effort. "I wrote a letter to God," she announced proudly. "It's about you. I didn't know what postage to put on it, so Grandpa said I could come over and ask."

"I just put one stamp on 'em," Ty said. "That seems to work fine." He turned back to the TV. "I'm watching cartoons."

"I like cartoons," Sam said. She reached over and took his hand. She noticed how white he was. And his hand was so cold.

Sam and her grandfather stayed long enough to watch a couple of cartoons. Once they left, Ty went up to bed and Maddy went out to her swing in the garden arbor. The night was crisp and clear with a million stars scattered overhead like diamonds on black velvet. Lost in thought, she didn't hear Brady until he was only a step away.

"Your mother let me in—" He started to speak but she couldn't wait to say what was on her heart.

"I'm so sorry," she said. She felt it so deeply but the words sounded so lame.

"No, no," Brady insisted. "That's all right. Don't worry about it. I just wanted to let you know Walter Finley is coming back next week. You'll have your old mailman again. But I feel so lucky that I've gotten to know you—your family, I mean."

Maddy held up her hand. "Please. I want to show you something." He followed her to a ladder leaning against the house and climbed up. Crabbing along the roof to keep their balance, they came to the fort outside Ty's window and sat down.

"Do you think this will hold us both?" Brady asked, smiling.

There was a beautiful view from Ty's private perch. The stars seemed even brighter than they had looked from the ground, and the shadows of the trees danced in the moonlight, their leaves swaying in the breeze. In the distance a church steeple pointed skyward, and the light inside it cast a soft glow over nearby rooftops.

"You can see everything from here," Maddy said, taking it all in. "You feel closer to God. I understand now that he wasn't just writing letters. He was praying. Just like Patrick did when he wrote." She looked at Brady. "I was wrong to treat you the way I did. I'm sorry I took it out on you."

"Don't give it another thought. I'm the one who should apologize." They sat for a moment, each lost in their own feelings. Then Brady pulled a letter out of his pocket.

"I have one more letter to deliver. I think he'd want you to read it."

She studied the envelope, started to open it, and then stopped. "I can't read this right now."

"That's all right. Just hang onto it."

"What we need more than anything is to feel like a normal family again, even for a little while," Maddy said. "No more hospitals, no more IVs, no more sickness. We just need to laugh again like old times."

Maddy got her wish, if only briefly, when the whole family was treated to a week at Give Kids the World Village in Orlando. Ty didn't stand out or feel self-conscious for a single minute because all the guests of honor were very sick children just as he was, all needing some degree of special care and attention. This was a rare chance for the kids to feel normal and for their parents to relax, knowing they were in expert hands.

Every day at the Village was built around whatever Ty wanted to do, whatever he wanted to eat, wherever he wanted to go. He and the family even had a hostess named Pamela, who was there to make sure he was having a good time and that everything he wished for was coming true. There was a movie theater just for kids, miniature golf, horseback riding, a playground, an ice cream parlor, a swimming pool, and almost anything else a kid could imagine—all free for the child and his family, including meals and a storybook chalet to live in.

Ty spent most of his time in a wheelchair now with Ben his proud companion and power source. Toward the middle of one morning, Pamela met Ty and Ben on the street that ran through Give Kids the World Village.

"Hey, Tyler. Hi, Ben. Another hot fudge breakfast?"

"Yep," Ty reported happily, holding it up. "Third day in a row. And I'm going to have two banana splits for lunch."

"Good for you," Pamela said.

"Miss Pamela, I need to mail this letter," Ty told her, handing it up.

"I'll be glad to take care of that," she offered. Then she read the address. "Wow! I'm going to have to find a special mailbox for this one."

"No," Ty reassured her, "any mailbox works."

"Okay, we'll see. Are you coming to the talent show tonight?"

"You bet. Ben and I are singing."

"No way!" Ben said, caught off guard. "I'm not singing!"

"Yes, you are!" Ty whooped as Ben spun his wheelchair around and around. "Stop it! You *are* singing! You *are*!"

"I am not getting up there in front of all those people!" Ben insisted, pushing Ty along.

"Bye, Miss Pamela," Ty squealed as they disappeared.

Pamela looked at the letter in her hand. "Good-bye, Tyler," she said softly.

When the Doherty brothers' turn came that night at the talent show, Ben rolled Ty onstage and strapped on his guitar. Ty rose slowly to his feet and scanned the audience. There were his mom and Granna; Sam was waving shamelessly with both hands, standing with her grandfather. Ty kept looking. Where was Brady? No sign of him.

Ben started strumming the intro. "My brother wrote this song," Ty announced, then began to sing:

I look at your smiling face.
You're so weak and yet you have such strength,
You take a glance around this place,
And you make the best of everything.

A few lines in, his voice started to falter. Despite his vow not to, Ben joined in to help fill out the sound. As Ty struggled to keep going, he saw Brady enter the room and felt a surge of energy.

You give me hope in spite of everything,
You show me love even with so much pain,
So I'll take this life and live like I was given another try.
We laugh, we cry,
Sometimes we're broken and we don't know why.
I'm tired and I lose my way.
You help me find faith.

The boys finished strong as the crowd erupted in applause.

Confetti came streaming down on them as Ty sank back into his wheelchair. To everyone's surprise, Brady walked to the stage and motioned for quiet.

"I don't mean to interrupt," Brady said, feeling awkward. "I'm not very good at this stuff. My name is Brady McDaniels, and I've been Tyler's mail carrier for the last couple of months. I just want all of you to know what a gift Tyler has been to me, and to all the people he has touched through his letters to God. I read a bunch of them. I'm not sure I was supposed to, but I think I was. Because I see now that there's more to this life than I could see. More than I ever imagined." He made eye contact with Maddy, Sam, Mr. Perryfield, and last of all Ty. "He gave me hope that even I might know what it means to have faith in something. To have faith in God."

Brady signaled to the back of the room. Lester Stevens, Carl Landers, and a line of other postal workers paraded up to the front with bag after bag of letters and set them in front of Ty's wheelchair at the edge of the stage. "These are all letters to God. You did this, Tyler. You not only helped me, you helped all these people, and many more people we don't even know about, find the *truth*."

Kneeling, Brady plunged his hands into one of the bags and came up with two handfuls of letters. Tyler took them from him and held them up for the crowd to see. The cheers almost raised the roof.

"This big bag here," Brady continued, pointing. "All these letters are from your school. Two hundred letters to God. You think you can handle delivering all these?"

"Yeah," Ty answered, exhausted but elated. "'Cause I'm God's warrior!"

≈

A very few days later, a brave young warrior's battle was drawing to a close. Ty lay still in his bed, his mother holding one hand and Brady holding the other. Ben and Granna were there too, all of them praying with a passion that was somehow serene at the same time. On the bedside table, Patrick's Bible, covered with his notes and underlines, lay open to a page from Second Corinthians.

"Hey, Tiger," Brady said in a husky voice, leaning close, "God told me he's been reading your letters and he can't wait to see you."

"Mommy," Tyler said gently, looking at her. His eyes were the only things that moved.

"You can let go now, precious one," she whispered through her tears. "I love you so much."

Ty moved his hands together until his mother's and Brady's hands touched, smiled a transcendent smile, and closed his eyes for the last time.

It was only later that Maddy could bring herself to read that final letter.

Dear God,

I think we did it. You told me not to be afraid and I wasn't, because you were with me all the time. I just want everybody to believe. I know you're real.

Love,

Tyler

Hearing the news, Sam hung up the phone and crawled into her grandpa's lap. She hugged him harder than she'd ever hugged him in her life. He hugged back, fishing again for his handkerchief. Later that night Sam wrote a letter of her own.

Dear God,

Tyler was the best friend ever. I didn't get to tell him, but when we prayed for Alex I asked you to come into my heart too. I know now I have forever-lasting life.

Word quickly spread up and down Laurel Lane—to Linda Baker, not long before she held up their newborn son to her soldier husband, home safe at last. "Jim, meet your son, Tyler James Baker." To Walter Finley and Erin Miller, who sat in Erin's porch swing, laughing and crying together late into the night. To people who loved the little boy at 244 Laurel Lane, and people who hardly knew him at all.

Joe Grundy didn't like being the new guy at the post office. He didn't know people's names, didn't know the routine, and especially didn't know what to do with a strange handful of letters he'd collected the first morning on his route. Weaving his way through the busy corridors, he made it to Lester Stevens' office. Brady McDaniels was standing in the doorway.

"Hey, Mr. Stevens," Joe said, "this really takes the cake. Look at these, would ya? Must be a dozen of them. Letters to God. What do I do with these?"

Brady and Lester exchanged knowing glances.

"I'll take this one," Lester volunteered.

"Great, thanks," Brady said. "I gotta go anyway."

Brady sped off to Give Kids the World Village, where there

was a very special celebration under way. He spotted Maddy in the big crowd and stood beside her. The whole street was packed.

"Sorry I'm late."

"Thanks for being here," Maddy said, giving his hand a squeeze.

"Can you believe it's been a year?" Brady asked.

"It doesn't seem possible."

Pastor Andy stood up front and signaled for quiet.

"How could a seven-year-old kid pierce the hearts of so many people?" he began. "He showed us, in a way nobody else could, that God is always doing what's best for us, even when it seems impossible. He reminded us that if everything were easy and obvious, we wouldn't need faith in our lives. Thank you, God, for Tyler's life. He helped us know that you always listen and always answer, even though it may not be the answer we wanted or the way we expected. And we're here today to celebrate his life by encouraging the whole world to write letters to God, starting right here, right now."

Andy signaled to Ben, who took a letter out of his pocket and held it high. Dozens and dozens of kids in the audience, and probably more than a few adults, held up letters of their own. Then Ben led everyone with a letter to a shiny new mailbox mounted nearby. The sign on the box said: "Tyler's Mailbox—Letters to God."

You yourselves are our letter, written on our hearts,
known and read by everybody.
2 Corinthians 3:2

Share Your Thoughts

With the Author: Your comments will be forwarded to the author when you send them to *zauthor@zondervan.com.*

With Zondervan: Submit your review of this book by writing to *zreview@zondervan.com.*

Free Online Resources at

www.zondervan.com

Zondervan AuthorTracker: Be notified whenever your favorite authors publish new books, go on tour, or post an update about what's happening in their lives at www.zondervan.com/authortracker.

Daily Bible Verses and Devotions: Enrich your life with daily Bible verses or devotions that help you start every morning focused on God. Visit www.zondervan.com/newsletters.

Free Email Publications: Sign up for newsletters on Christian living, academic resources, church ministry, fiction, children's resources, and more. Visit www.zondervan.com/newsletters.

Zondervan Bible Search: Find and compare Bible passages in a variety of translations at www.zondervanbiblesearch.com.

Other Benefits: Register yourself to receive online benefits like coupons and special offers, or to participate in research.

ZONDERVAN.com/
AUTHORTRACKER
follow your favorite authors